Ghosted

Allyson Charles

Chapter One

THE EXHAUST PIPE OF the monstrous pick-up truck drifted toward her front bumper, spewing black fumes like a thirty-pack a week dragon. Bridget's hand hovered over her steering wheel, just twitching to horn the guy. Seriously, who needed a truck that big? She'd need a stepladder to crawl into it.

The truck drifted back into its own lane, and Bridget swallowed, the back of her throat raw. Her uncle would have said that was a her-problem. That just because she was vertically-challenged didn't mean the rest of the world had to accommodate her. Then he would have ruffled her hair, called her a shrimp, and blasted her with his wide, honest smile.

She would have pretended to be annoyed, but secretly reveled in his open affection.

Bridget blinked, trying to make the traffic around her come into focus. She'd never get to fake her irritation at her outrageous uncle again. Never hear his burly laugh. Never listen as he described what went into making the perfect hamburger for the zillionth time.

He was gone.

The truck edged over the dotted white line. Bridget gripped the steering wheel. And she could be just as gone if she didn't pay attention to this yahoo on the road. His truck could roll right over her Ford Pinto without even feeling a bump.

She rolled down her window, a good Irish tongue-lashing at the ready, before she remembered her vow to clean up her language. She blew out a breath as the hot and humid North Carolina air invaded her car.

Her uncle had always said the air in the south felt like a hug, welcoming you.

Bridget thought it felt more like a boa constrictor. The only thing she'd missed about the south when her family had moved had been her uncle.

"Dude, stay in your lane," she muttered as the truck drifted away from her, inching into the lane on the other side. She snorted at the irony of her telling someone to stay in his lane. It had been one of the last things Kevin had said to her before cutting off communication. But when there was an actual, physical lane, she'd forgive herself. The road was the only place that comment was allowed.

The light ahead turned yellow, and she happily stepped on the brake as the truck blasted past to make it through the intersection, leaving her at the red light. Jacksonville was a moderately-sized city, not quite 80,000 citizens, but at this time of day, the traffic was starting to thicken. Compared to Southern California, however, it was like a drive in the park.

Her phone buzzed from the passenger seat. Bridget snatched it up, but let loose a long breath when she saw it was just a spam text. Kevin was still ignoring her texts. And her calls. And emails. Two years together and now nothing.

A purple muscle car rolled to a stop next to her. The thrum of the engine hit Bridget low in the belly. The thing probably ate gas like she did cookies when the Girl Scouts came around. Why were men so impractical when it came to their cars? That had been something else she and Kevin had argued about. He'd wanted to lease a BMW. She'd wanted to save money for a house.

The car next to her started blasting Sammy Hagar's "I Can't Drive 55." The good-looking man driving it tapped the wheel and sang along, his voice drowned out by the radio. It would almost be cute, how into the song the guy was if she hadn't just lived through the worst couple of weeks of her life. *He* would almost be cute. The man had short, dark hair, luscious caramel skin, and shoulders that she could tell, even between two windows, stretched for miles.

But she *had* been living through the past couple of weeks. Through the news of her uncle's death, his memorial service the family had held in California, the talks with the attorney. Getting fired. Getting dumped. It was no longer in her to find anything cute.

So when the light turned green and Mr. Can't Drive 55 cut in front of her, only remembering to put on his turn signal halfway into her lane, she didn't hold back. She leaned on her horn.

A sad *beep beeeep* burbled from her Pinto. She wanted her honk to match her mood, angry and with no more fucks to give. She wanted the honk of a semi-truck. Instead she got the sound the Roadrunner might make if he were hungover.

She hit the horn again, willing her displeasure to be made known to everyone around her.

The driver in the purple car merely tossed her a casual wave and turned right at the next intersection.

"Ass muncher," Bridget muttered, her knuckles going white around the wheel. The man was going her way. She thought about following, giving him a piece of her mind.

But sanity, and the low-fuel indicator blinking frantically up at her from the dash, eased her foot off the accelerator.

"Okay, Gimli." She patted the dash of her car. "Let's get you some food. We can't both be running on empty."

Ten minutes later, fully fueled and feeling slightly better after the gas station candy bar, Bridget pulled into a familiar, and crowded, parking lot. She stepped onto the asphalt, the toe of her black, canvas shoe sinking into a pothole. She stared at the bar. It had been almost ten years but it could have been yesterday. Same weathered metal roof. Same wooden porch with inviting red doors.

But no Uncle Kieran.

She picked at a thread on the cuff of her black suit jacket. This pant suit was the only one she owned, and the only thing even close to being appropriate for a memorial. Black washed out her skin tone and made her hair look Bozo the Clown levels of orange, but she'd never cared much about her appearance before. Now definitely wasn't the time to start.

She plodded to the entrance of *The Limber Ginger* and pushed inside. A mass of people, in everything from shorts and flip flops to three-piece suits, milled about, drinks in hand, as a woman on a small stage in the corner of the bar spoke about Kieran Kennedy. Her voice was amplified through the bar's sound system, letting everyone hear the tears in her voice.

Bridget found Karen Matthews, Kieran's assistant manager, nursing a hot coffee on a stool at the bar.

"Karen." Bridget stuck out her hand. "It's good to finally meet you in person." The video calls they'd made hadn't done the woman justice. She'd known the woman was middle-aged, attractive, with dark hair, but she hadn't been able to tell through the internet connection how expressive Karen's eyes were. Filled with humor and intelligence.

Bridget's shoulders relaxed. Maybe she shouldn't be so quick to judge by appearances, but she had a feeling the two of them would get along well.

They shook, Karen's hand warm from cupping her mug.

"Yes, much better than talking over the internet." Karen gave her a wan smile. "Although I wish it were under different circumstances."

Someone jostled into Bridget, and she huddled closer to the bar. "This is quite a turn out for the memorial of a bar owner. Uncle Kieran would have loved it."

"Everyone loved Kieran, customers and staff alike." Karen raised one shoulder. "The discounted drinks don't hurt, either. You're starting your ownership of the *Ginger* running a loss."

"Tomorrow I can worry about making a profit." Bridget scanned the bar, her insides churning. She'd never owned anything worth more than her car. And her car hadn't been expensive even when it had been new. She was good with numbers but what did she know about running a business? She'd always had someone else signing her paycheck.

"Who's that?" Bridget asked, pointing at the woman finishing up her speech on the low stage. "She seems to be taking my uncle's death hard."

"Patricia Nealy. Patty. She's a waitress here. She and Kieran were especially tight."

Bridget arched an eyebrow.

"Not like that." Karen huffed a laugh. "But Kieran helped her through a rough time. He helped a lot of us." She swallowed. "He'll be missed."

And Bridget had extremely large shoes to fill. She pressed her palms to the cool wood bar, focusing on the swirl of the wood grain. Uncle Kieran thought she could do it. The letter he'd included with his will had made that clear. He hadn't even considered the idea that she might sell.

And she wouldn't. *The Limber Ginger* had been too big a part of his life to do that. Too big a part of her own childhood. Even if she'd still been employed, still been with Kevin, she would have found a way to make it work.

But Uncle Kieran had fallen off a ladder at exactly the right time in her life to make her decision easy.

The bar in front of her blurred.

Damn the man for dying.

"A whiskey tonic, please," a deep male voice said next to her.

"What label do you want?" the bartender asked.

"Kieran would have been offended if I drank anything other than Irish." The man leaned his arms on the bar, the elbow of his light-blue, long-sleeved shirt resting close to Bridget's hand. "Jamieson."

"Redbreast," she corrected automatically. "If you're going to be drinking to my uncle, it should be with the best. On the house," she added, not wanting to stick the guy with the upcharge.

The bartender looked at her, then to Karen, who gave a small nod.

Oh yeah. No one here knew who she was, except for the assistant manager. She'd have to schedule a staff meeting. Her uncle had been amazing managing his employees.

Most of them had been like family to him. Would she be able to earn the same respect?

"You're the niece?" The surprise in the man's voice almost had her smiling. Not many people had believed she and her uncle were related, especially not when they stood side by side. Bridget had come from a family of veritable giants, and she was the runt of the litter.

"Bridget Sullivan." She turned, looked up a good ten inches before meeting his eyes. She stuck out her hand. "Thank you for coming...." Her voice trailed off. She squinted. The jaw line. The strong nose. "You cut me off," she said, accusing.

Before she could pull her hand back, he engulfed it with his own. "I didn't say anything." He cocked his head.

"Not verbally. On the road today, coming here." She frowned. Close up, he was even more handsome. She'd spent time around a lot of athletes, but this man's body was insane. The broad shoulders of a swimmer, a trim waist, and muscles everywhere in between.

She sniffed. Probably thought he was entitled to everything, including road lanes.

"I don't cut people off." He dropped her hand. "You must have mistaken me for another driver."

"Gas guzzling purple hot rod?" She rolled up onto her toes, hoping to gain an inch or two against him. "I even horned you. Didn't you hear me?"

He grinned, his teeth white against his olive skin. "The 1978 Pinto in Ford Tangerine. You were angry honking? I couldn't tell with that cute little *beep beep*. I thought you were saying hello."

She pressed her lips together. She was going to upgrade her horn. "Regardless, you cut me off."

"Your whiskey tonic, sir." The bartender garnished the glass with lemon and handed it across the bar.

"I gave you a good fifteen feet." He reached for the drink.

"Men always overestimate distances. And sizes." And because liars didn't deserve top shelf, she snatched the drink from the bartender before Mr. Hot Rod could enjoy it.

His eyebrows shot up as another patron bumped into her from behind. She jerked forward, the whiskey and tonic sloshing over the rim.

And splashing right onto the front of his neatly-pressed, button-down shirt.

She stared at the wet patch, her shoulders sagging. Wasn't that just the way her life was going? Nothing was neat. Or easy. "Son of a—"

Chapter Two

THE COLD LIQUOR WAS sticky against his abdomen. Tony dropped his gaze and stared at the wet patch that covered a large portion of his shirt. His freshly-pressed shirt.

Perfect. Just perfect. He grabbed the napkins the bartender handed him and did what he could. It wasn't much.

The redhead in front of him sighed, staring into the now-empty glass. "What a waste."

"Yeah, this is only the second time I've worn this shirt." He tossed the sodden napkins onto the bar. And Melissa had said she liked him in blue.

The woman, Bridget, she'd said, frowned. "The shirt? I was talking about the whiskey." She lifted the tumbler to her mouth and ran her tongue around the rim.

Tony blinked. He was military, surrounded by rude, crude men day in and day out. Poor manners weren't new to him. But something about the easy dismissal of the destruction of one of his best shirts, combined with her *licking* his glass, was appalling.

He stared as she flicked her tongue a little deeper down the glass, trying to salvage the last drop. His lower belly tensed. Okay, it was a little bit sexy, too. But mainly appalling.

Karen leaned around the redhead and grimaced. "I might have a hairdryer in the back."

"No, thanks." Tony gave a head bob to his fellow Marine Raider, Ryan Kelly, as he entered the bar and headed to their table in the corner. "I've got another one in my car."

Karen nudged Bridget, giving her a meaningful look before nodding at Tony.

Bridget's eyebrows drew together. "What?"

"You said you might need help on the customer service side of the business," Karen hissed. "This is your chance."

Bridget glanced back up at Tony, a baffled look on her face.

An apology didn't seem to be forthcoming. "Whatever." He turned and pushed through the crowd, heading for the exit. Heated whispers followed after him, before fading away.

He paused outside the door, raising his face to the waning afternoon sun. He and his squad had just returned stateside two days ago from a mission that had ended messy. He still hadn't fully adjusted to civilian life. Finding out their favorite bar owner had passed while they'd been gone hadn't helped. They thought they were the ones who faced all the danger when they left on their ops. But people still lived and died back home.

The door behind him exploded open, and a tiny package of black rayon and ginger hair tumbled toward him.

Instinctively, he grabbed her shoulders, setting her up straight.

"New company rule," she called back through the closing door. "No pushing."

"Are you all right?" he asked. Out of the dim light of the bar, he could see more of her features. A smattering of freckles across a cute button-nose. Wide-set amber eyes fringed with thick lashes. A plush mouth that gave a man too many ideas.

He dragged his gaze back to her eyes.

"Fine." She stepped back. "But I have been informed that I might owe you an apology. And perhaps money to clean your shirt." She shoved her hands in the front pockets of her slacks. The lapels of her suit jacket gaped open with the movement, revealing a mustard yellow T-shirt. *What Doesn't Kill You Gives You XP* was written across it in black ink, over the backdrop of a stylized dragon.

He forced his mind away from wondering what the hell XP was. "Apology accepted." Turning, he strode for his car.

She trotted after him. "I'm not great with social manners, but I think this is where you then apologize for cutting me off this afternoon."

"But I didn't cut you off." He pulled his keys from his pocket and unlocked his trunk.

"You did so." She nudged his tire with the toe of her canvas sneaker. "Why do guys feel the need to waste money on cars like these? You can't get much more than ten miles per gallon."

He unzipped the duffel bag inside and dug through it, looking for his spare dress shirt. Socks, undershirts, workout clothes.... "Sheila may like to eat, but she has other compensations. She's a 1970 Plymouth Barracuda and worth every penny in gas." Nothing felt as good as putting his foot on the pedal and *going*.

"I hope she's worth crazy high insurance and repair costs, too." Bridget peered around him, the top of her curls barely reaching his shoulder. "You keep a whole other wardrobe in your car?"

"I like to be prepared." He found the button-down and unrolled it. A couple wrinkles, but not too bad. "You know, for when women throw drinks on me."

"Happens a lot, does it?"

He slid his sports coat off and handed it to her, before working on the buttons of his shirt. "First time anyone's actually directed it at me, but I do sometimes get caught in the cross-fire." Ryan was the one who should keep a spare wardrobe in his car. He pissed off women left and right.

Her mouth dropped open as he stripped from the ruined shirt and slid on the new one.

"So, you're the new owner of the *Ginger*, I take it?"

Her gaze followed the movement of his fingers as he buttoned up the shirt. "Huh? What's that?"

"The bar." He nodded to the building. "You're Kieran's niece and the assistant manager was deferring to you. You're the new owner."

"Yes." She shook her head and shoved his jacket at him. "Yeah. *The Limber Ginger* is now mine."

He locked the trunk, and they turned back for the bar. "Well, I hope you don't sell to a developer," he said. "My friends love this place."

"But not you?"

"It's fine." He looked down at her shrewd expression. "It's a good place to unwind," he conceded. But it wasn't the type of place he'd feel comfortable taking a date. He could only imagine Melissa's face if he brought her here.

But Bridget had just lost her uncle. He didn't need to tell her the bar she'd inherited was a bit of a dive. Besides, she had to already know.

He grabbed the handle to the door but didn't open it. "I didn't tell you yet. I'm sorry about your uncle. He was a good man."

She looked down at her feet. "Thank you. He was an even better uncle."

His hand twitched. Just for an instant, he wanted to reach out to her. Provide some sort of comfort. But the crazy thought disappeared as quickly as it had come. He opened the door and ushered her inside.

They paused on the threshold. He shifted his weight. "Well, my group is over there." He pointed to the large round table filled with his friends.

She nodded. "And I should probably say something." She nodded to the stage. "No one here but Karen knows who I am. And you."

"Yes." The silence stretched between them.

She fidgeted with her weird T-shirt.

He forced himself not to still her hand. This was a meeting he didn't need to repeat, but he was oddly reluctant to leave.

"Okay, then." She flashed him a smile and gave an awkward wave of her hand. "See you around...." The skin between her eyebrows wrinkled.

"Tony," he filled in. "Anthony Garcia, but my friends call me Tony."

"Actually, we like to call you asshat, swabbie, or bullet sponge." A moron in a green-checked shirt stepped next to him, a shit-eating grin on his face. "Rarely Tony."

Tony cracked his neck. "Travis, this is Kieran's niece, Bridget. Maybe keep the stupid jokes to yourself this time?"

His squad mate's face sobered. "Sorry, Bridget. We really do miss your uncle."

She grinned. "Nothing to apologize for. He made this bar for swabbies and bullet sponges. Though he had a low tolerance for asshats. Sorry, Tony, but my uncle probably cared for you about as much as you care for this bar."

Tony narrowed his eyes.

She shrugged. "Them's the breaks."

Travis threw back his head and laughed. "If you have time, you should come by our table, have a drink with us. I want the rest of the guys to meet Kieran's famous niece."

Her cheeks flushed red. "Oh, God, my uncle always talked me up too much. People have high expectations when they meet me and I always disappoint."

"He loved you," Tony said.

"Yeah." She blinked rapidly. Nodding to Travis, she said, "Thanks for coming. I'll see you guys around." And she slid between two patrons and disappeared from sight.

"Hey, I'm heading to the bar," Travis said. "Want something?"

"No, I'm good." And he didn't have another back-up shirt. "I have to leave in twenty anyway. I have a date."

"Got it." Travis headed in the direction Bridget had gone.

Tony dragged his feet in the other direction, toward their table. He wished he wasn't on a deadline, that he could just relax with his friends tonight. He rolled his shoulders. He needed to get out of this post-mission funk. Melissa would be expecting him to be his usual charming self.

He'd been looking forward to this date all day, but for the life of him, he couldn't remember why.

Chapter Three

THE SKY WAS MOLTEN silver as she entered the drive to her uncle's house. The bottoms of the dark clouds undulated like mercury, seeming to laugh with contempt at each jounce of her car on the rutted drive. For a man who spent his life surrounded by people at his bar, her Uncle Kieran sure seemed to love his privacy when he went home at night.

Bridget bumped around a curve hemmed in tight with thick brambles before the house came into view. A small shiver whispered down her spine. Kieran's home could never have been considered charming in the best of times, but now, after a month of neglect, the place looked downright homely. Two stories, with a low-hung attic whose two small, round windows seemed to glare down at her darkly. The green paint on the house was so faded as to be nonexistent in parts, exposing the rough timber below. Her uncle had detested yard work, and weeds crept up to the porch steps, looking as though they only waited for the order to launch an invasion of the house. The one nice feature was the porch that wrapped all the way around the house.

She parked her car under the standalone steel carport and sighed. The house was her brother's now, but since he was letting her stay here rent-free while she got herself sorted, she felt some obligation to clean it up for its inevitable sale.

She hated yardwork as much as her uncle. And house repairs. And painting. Her mouth twisted wryly. She'd have to get over it. She didn't live in a swanky condo now, nor have a nine-to-five office job. She'd have to get her hands dirty if she wanted to survive.

Grabbing her bags, she plodded to the house as thunder rumbled overhead. She'd bought some groceries on her way home, and she was bringing the last of them in as the first fat drops of rain began to fall. She kicked the front door closed and sagged back against it.

It had been a day. Trying to be social at the memorial when her own heart was breaking had been a special sort of challenge. And then meeting all of the employees, *her* employees now, had left her wiped. What if she screwed up, went bankrupt, and all those people lost their jobs? Her uncle had thought of them as family. She couldn't disappoint him.

She brought everything to the kitchen, glad that at least this room had been remodeled within the last decade. The stove, dishwasher, and refrigerator all matched, and were only a couple of years old. The cabinets were glass-fronted, and showed a hodge-podge of plates and glasses that looked homey rather than cluttered. And the sink, well, she could bathe a German Shepard in the farm-style sink it was so big.

She dismissed the thought of getting a dog. Kevin hadn't liked them (which should have been her first clue), but as satisfying as it would be to start doing all the things she'd wanted to but hadn't because of him, it wouldn't be fair to the poor animal at this point. She needed to get settled first.

To that end, she grabbed a bucket and some cleaning supplies and got to work. Her mom had said she'd trusted Bridget to sort out which of Kieran's personal belongings to give away or keep, and if there was any doubt, she'd send pictures of the items.

It was late into the night before she finally decided to call it quits. She sagged into the leather couch and glared at the living room. The overhead light was off, but the small lamp on the end table gave off enough of a glow to show that the shelves in the room were now empty and dust-free. The cupboards that ran along three of the walls, however, were still cluttered with every DVD known to mankind. Kieran had even kept some VHS tapes, even though she had yet to find a player. He'd loved his movies, and for some reason, boxing up and getting rid of that part of him sent a dull ache through her chest.

The summer she'd spent with him as a teenager had been filled with evenings curled up on this couch with him, laughing and throwing popcorn at the monster classics he'd tried to get her to love as much as he had.

She dropped her head to the backrest and stared at the ceiling. Her eyes blurred. From exhaustion. From missing Kieran. From the destruction of her former life. She let her body meld with the leather beneath her and just *was*.

She didn't know how long the light had been gathering along the ceiling before she finally noticed. She rubbed her eyes. It had a dancing quality, less like light and more like tiny embers that gathered and spun near the ceiling. They seemed to coalesce, take shape, and a shiver raced down her spine.

Her mother used to tell her ghost stories. Ghost stories, and tales about selkies and fairies and banshees. It had been Bridget's reward for getting ready for bed, although it had made her sleep with a nightlight until she was fourteen years old. She hadn't believed the stories, not really, and she wasn't going to start believing in things that went bump in the night now, either.

So when the wood on the front porch groaned, sounding all too much like what she imagined the groan of a banshee would be as it heralded the death of a family member, she calmly rose and made her way to the front entry.

It took her shaking fingers only two attempts to find the light switch beside the front door.

But when she finally threw on the porch light and peered through the window, no one was there.

Chapter Four

"HEY, KAREN." BRIDGET WIPED her forehead with the bandana tied around her wrist. "Were you looking for something in the office?" She'd almost said Uncle Kieran's office. It still didn't feel like it was her own.

Late morning sunlight filtered in from all the open windows. She and Karen and a couple of the staff were giving the bar a thorough cleaning, something that had been neglected for quite a while. There was something about cleaning, about putting things to order in the bright light of day to erase any lingering fancies one might have entertained about ghosts and goblins.

Karen looked up from the base of a table she was dusting. "Not recently. Why?"

"A couple of things have been moved." She chewed her bottom lip. Another staff member had probably been looking for a pen or something. Still, the safe was back there, and the personal information of the employees. She was going to have to be more security-conscious.

Karen cracked her neck. "Weird. Hey, did you have a chance to look over the budget reports I gave you?"

"Yes, thanks for pulling that together." At least one thing was going right. *The Limber Ginger* was making a profit. Nothing earth-shattering, but enough for a comfortable living if she managed it right.

With a grimace, she picked up the pot of soapy water and a rag she'd left on the bar. She really wanted to delegate this job to someone else. Cleaning baseboards was the worst. But what kind of leadership would that show?

She paused in front of a section of wall. Twinkle lights ringed the ceiling of the bar, and the strand above her was dark. She swallowed. "Is this where it happened?" she asked quietly.

Karen grabbed the edge of the table and pulled herself upright. She twisted the rag in her hands. "Yes. I told the old fool to make one of the younger guys get up on that ladder. He just laughed." She planted a hand on her generous hip. "I can't believe he tried to change that strand after hours when no one was around to hold the ladder. I mean, I can believe it, he was always doing things like that, but I wish he was here so I could give him a piece of my mind."

"Yeah." Bridget's lips turned upwards even as she blinked back tears. That was her Uncle Kieran. "Well." She cleared her throat. "Something else to add to my to-do list." Then she knelt and started scrubbing. She'd made it halfway around the room when a pair of blue ballet flats edged into her vision.

"Hi, Bridget. Can we talk for a sec?"

"Gladly." Bridget rose and stretched her back. She eyed the twenty-something woman in front of her. "Patty, right?" *The Limber Ginger* had thirteen employees, and Bridget had used every memory trick she knew to remember all their names. She'd only been semi-successful so far.

The woman toyed with the end of her sleek sable ponytail. "Yeah. Um, I'm scheduled to work this afternoon, but I was hoping to switch shifts."

"Again?" Karen strolled over. "That's the third time this month."

Patty lifted her chin. "I have to move again. And my friend who has a truck can only help me this afternoon. And—"

"It's fine." Bridget raised her hand. "I can cover it."

Karen and Patty glanced at each other. "Uh, have you ever waited tables before?" Karen asked.

"Yes, in this very bar." She'd spent the summer with her uncle one year in high school, and he hadn't been shy about putting her to work. She'd only been allowed to serve food, but drinks couldn't be that much harder. "Besides, I should do everyone's job at least once. Really get a feel for the business."

"Thanks." Patty backed quickly away, as though afraid she'd change her mind. "I'll see you guys tomorrow." She gave a quick wave before hightailing it out the door.

Karen sighed. "I feel for the girl, really I do. But reliable she is not."

"She was the waitress who gave that speech about my uncle." Bridget headed behind the bar and spritzed soda water into a glass. She dropped a wedge of lime in it. "What's her story?" She held up an empty glass, and Karen nodded. Bridget filled it and handed it over.

"She's nice enough, but an idiot when it comes to men. Always picking losers." Karen downed her water and handed it over for a refill. "The last one was abusive, I think. Kieran tried to help her. Gave her some money to move out from the guy's place. Would always walk her to her car. That sort of thing."

Bridget frowned. "Do you think she's moving back in with him?"

"I hope not, but it's really not my business."

Bridget's phone vibrated in her back pocket. She pulled it out and bit back an oath. *Speaking of jerks.* "Kevin. So nice of you to finally get back to me."

"I don't have time for your sarcasm." Her ex's voice oozed over the line. It was a deep voice that she'd once found sexy. Now it just raised her hackles. "Where is it?"

Bridget swallowed the last of her water, wishing it was something stronger. "Where's what?"

"Don't play that game. You took one of the company's external hard drives. Unless you want the police at your door, you'll send it back."

Karen planted one butt cheek on a barstool, not bothering to even try to look like she wasn't listening.

Bridget gripped her glass. "You've been ignoring my messages for a month now and this is why you call? To accuse me of theft?" *Un-flipping-believable.*

"You're lucky I'm calling instead of sending someone to your door."

Bridget's shoulders drew back. "I don't know what you're talking about, Kevin. The only thing I left your dad's company with was a shred of dignity and a whole lot of anger." She wasn't sure about the dignity bit, but it sounded nice to say. It had been hard to keep any semblance of grace when she'd basically been frog-marched out of the company's building by security five minutes after learning she'd been fired.

His voice went low and mean. "We want those files back. And if you show them to anyone, *anyone*, you're going to be in a lot more trouble than with just the police."

Bridget pulled the phone away from her ear and stared at it. The name Kevin Carhart lit the display, an image she'd seen thousands of times before. Seeing his name on her phone used to bring her joy. It was surreal hearing threats from him now.

"What's up?" Karen whispered.

Slowly, Bridget shook her head. Kevin, and by extension his father, thought she'd taken the files she'd brought to their attention. Her stomach clenched. She'd thought she was being helpful bringing the irregularities she'd found to them. Now she knew why she was actually fired. "You and your dad were up to some shifty shit, weren't you?" she said, bringing the phone back to her ear.

Karen arched an eyebrow as she slid off the stool. She walked to the end of the bar and grabbed an empty pickle jar. Written in blue capital letters on the masking tape wrapped around the glass were the words SWEAR JAR. She plopped it down in front of Bridget and pointed.

Bridget pressed her lips together. She'd told the assistant manager about her attempts to stop swearing. Karen had suggested the swear jar, the money going to a pizza party for the employees when it filled up.

It was going to fill fast. She dug in the pocket of her jeans as Kevin spluttered.

"You were an IT Manager," he said. "You never did understand finance. That's why we let you go. You couldn't—"

"Stay in my lane," she said along with him. She dropped a quarter in the jar. "It doesn't take an accountant to see that your numbers don't add up." And it shouldn't have taken her boyfriend firing her to see how wrong they were for each other. Kevin had been tailored suits and white wine. She was sneakers and whiskey. And all the hobbies she'd hid from him, too embarrassed to let him see how big a nerd he had in his bed, hadn't been healthy in a relationship, either.

Bile rose in her throat. And now it turned out she'd been sleeping with a crook. Probably. She didn't know what all Kevin and his father were up to, and she didn't care. She was on the other side of the country now. That part of her life was over. "Look, Kevin, I didn't take any files. I wanted you to send me that last box of my things, but I don't even care about that anymore. Don't call me again."

"I'll do whatever the hell I want," Kevin growled, and Bridget wondered how she had ever stomached hearing that voice whisper endearments in her ear. "And if we don't get the hard drive back, I won't just be calling. I'll be on your doorstep. And you won't like what I do to reclaim it."

A wave of heat rose from Bridget's chest, up her neck, and exploded across her face. "Is that a threat?" Two years. *Two years* she'd spent with this asshole. She'd thought they were going to marry. Have kids together. And now he was threatening her? Hell no.

She dug for every loose coin she had in her pocket and dumped them in the swear jar. Grabbing a bag of trash, she stomped out to the back alley as she told Kevin just what she thought. God, it felt good to unload on him. Shoving the phone between her ear and shoulder, she lifted the lid to the dumpster. "And another thing, you infantile, pathetic bit of rectum fungus, if you ever..."

The man rose from around the side of the dumpster. He was faceless, a baseball cap pulled low and the collar of his black windbreaker raised around his cheeks.

Bridget ignored the angry squawks coming through her phone, her pulse kicking up a beat. "Hi." She swallowed. "Do you need something? Are you hungry, because our kitchen is just starting to open." Was he a dumpster diver? The thought of anyone needing food that badly hurt.

He took a step toward her, and she fell back. He still hadn't spoken, but...that step hadn't been friendly. Bridget was a strong believer that a person's sixth sense was an accumulation of subconscious observations, and her subconscious was screaming at her that this dude was up to no good.

He took another step, and Bridget didn't hesitate. She threw the bag of trash at his head and sprinted for the door to the bar. It opened before she could reach it.

Bridget couldn't stop in time. She plowed into Karen who held two large plastic bags of her own. Karen's eyes flew wide, and then they were down, a tangle of limbs and liquor-soaked garbage.

"Up!" Bridget scrambled to her feet, her knee pressing into Karen's abdomen. "Get inside!"

Karen groaned. "My ovary."

Bridget grabbed Karen's arm and pulled her to her feet. She pushed her inside the bar, glancing over her shoulder to see how close the man was.

She stopped.

"What the hell?" Karen slapped her hands away. She peered over Bridget's shoulder. "Is there a rabid dog or something in the alley?"

"No." Bridget tried to slow her breathing. She took a tentative step back into the alley, looking up and down the narrow lane. Empty. "There was a man. I thought he was going to hurt me."

"Marcus!" Karen called back into the building. They waited until the burly cook lumbered to the door then followed as he investigated the alley. He picked up Bridget's phone that she'd dropped when she'd started running, tossed the bags of trash into the dumpster, and shrugged.

Bridget planted her hands on her hips and exhaled slowly. Had she overreacted? In the moment, she'd been certain the man was going to attack her. But looking back, she might have misread the situation. She might have scared the poor guy as much as he had her.

Her instincts still told her she'd been right to run.

It didn't matter. Just like the phantom of the night before, the man had vanished.

Chapter Five

Tony's opponent feinted left. Tony rolled onto the balls of his toes, the blue mat cool beneath his bare feet. This was almost unfair. His arm reach was almost twice the length of the shorter Marine's. He was all for training with other units, but maybe they should spar by height class—

The other man darted in, one arm wrapping around Tony's thigh, the other grabbing his arm. Before Tony could blink, he was flat on his back, staring up into Aldo's smiling face.

Aldo tutted. "You know what they say. The bigger they are...."

"The pissier they get when they fall." Chris Gunn, one of Tony's squad mates, swaggered up. He grabbed Tony's hand and pulled him up. "That's the second time you went down today. PMS?"

"That's not even funny to twelve year olds." Tony bumped his fist against the Marine's and watched as the kid swaggered off to his buddies. He took down someone from special forces. The young Marine would enjoy telling that story tonight.

"Seriously." Chris ran his fingers through his black hair. "Your head isn't in the game today. What's going on?"

"I know where his head is." Ryan Kelly, another member of their five-man squad, chucked a water bottle at him, then at Chris. Tony just barely got his hand up in time to catch it before it bounced off his forehead.

"Wasn't it date number three with that sexy blonde two nights ago?" Ryan continued. He plopped down on a weight bench and dragged a towel over his arms. "My head would be running over the highlight reel with that number, too."

The final two members of their squad drifted over from their own grappling match.

"Do lawyers even follow the three-date rule?" Travis asked. The little lines around his eyes and mouth that showed how much he liked to laugh deepened. "I'd think they'd throw in some extra regulations to slow the process down."

"No one follows the three-date rule." Tony dropped to a squat by his duffel bag and dug through it for his watch. He kept his head down as he snapped the Omega

Seamaster around his wrist. "It's an invention of teenage boys."

"For once the frogman and I agree." Ryan arched his blond eyebrows. "Can you imagine having to wait three dates to fuck?"

Chris heaved a sigh. "God must have a warped sense of humor. He gave you that innocent, baby-boy face yet so much depravity hides behind it. Thank heavens you have no interest in settling down. No woman should be inflicted with you."

Travis snorted. "Can you imagine the type of woman who would end up with Hawk long-term?" He asked, using Ryan's call sign. "Imagine him married?" Travis started to laugh. "God help the poor creature who gets leg-shackled to him."

Ryan scowled. "This Hawk's exceptional vision lets me see any woman who has designs past one night. I avoid 'em like gonorrhea. It will never happen."

Tony tuned out their chatter. With his luck, man-whore Ryan probably would settle down before Tony ever did. Ryan would need a personality change and for all the local ladies to have collective amnesia, but the chances of that seemed higher than Tony's own luck turning around.

"You all right?" The final member of their squad, Jake Skinner, stood in front of him, staring down with his eerie sea glass eyes. Their Element Leader, Jake felt a duty to check in on his men. Even if he hadn't led their squad, Jake "Psychic" Skinner was the kind of man who would intuit their problems and try to solve them.

Tony stood and uncapped his water. "Fine." He gave Jake a half-grin. "Why? You having a feeling?"

Jake looked toward the center mat, his eyes unfocused, his mouth grim.

"Oh shit. You do have a bad feeling." His hand clenched on the plastic bottle, making it crackle. When Jake had one of those feelings, shit was about to go sideways.

The other guys went silent, their attention now on Jake and Tony.

Tony tried to lighten the mood. "Well, it's not about me. Melissa and I decided to call it off. No biggie. We'd only seen each other a couple times."

After a sidelong glance at Jake, Chris forced a smile on his face and slapped Tony on the shoulder. "Why'd you do that? She checked all your boxes. Classy. Educated. Professional."

"Smokin' hot," Ryan added.

"We just didn't click." Tony shrugged. Melissa was almost...too perfect. Was that a thing? It couldn't be. No, the problem must lie in Tony. He saw all his friends settling down into committed relationships and he wanted the same. But he was always finding something wrong with the women he dated. And they were quality women. If his medical training leant to psychology, he'd say he was sabotaging his chances for some reason.

Ryan stretched. "I get that. Chemistry's important. It's like me and that new owner of the *Ginger*. Bridget, right? I think there was a definite spark there when she came by our table."

A slight burning sensation fizzled to life in Tony's stomach. He swallowed some more water. Probably that burrito he had for lunch.

"Only you would think about picking up a woman at her uncle's memorial," Jake said dryly. His dark mood seemed to have disappeared.

A Marine who looked like she was barely out of high school asked to use the weight machine behind him, and Jake scooted forward. "Let's hit the showers. You boys stink."

"And you smell like an Irish spring, I suppose?" Travis huffed but followed Jake toward the gym's door. The rest of them trailed behind.

Tony blinked when they stepped into the sunlight. It was another hot, humid day at Camp Lejeune in North Carolina. Coming from New York, he was used to hot and humid. He tugged at the collar of his tee shirt. Didn't mean he liked it.

Jake's phone buzzed in his bag and he pulled it out. His feet slowed. "We've got another review at oh nine hundred tomorrow. Price says someone from D.C. is going to be there."

Travis cursed. "We have drones killing families by mistake and no one high up even blinks. I shoot one terrorist who wasn't supposed to be there and they're crawling up my asshole."

Jake gripped his shoulder. "It was a good call. A good kill. The review will find that."

"We all have your back on this one," Tony added. "We couldn't let him leave with that Semtex. If you hadn't taken the shot, one of us would have."

Travis gripped the back of his neck. "Is this what your sixth sense is warning about?" he asked Jake. "Is my career ending?"

Jake slid his sunglasses on. "I don't know. I don't think so. Something else is coming."

"Great." Chris frowned. "And the hits keep coming."

"Come on, losers." Ryan walked backwards away from them. "Can we stop the whining and focus on the positives? *The Limber Ginger* tonight. Me. The new girl. You can live vicariously through my life and watch how an expert gets to home plate without having to go through three dates."

Tony rolled his eyes. He didn't see the new owner of the *Ginger* going for Ryan. She seemed too down-to-earth to put up with his friend's BS.

Travis groaned, but followed Ryan toward the showers. "The only thing I can learn from you is how to erase your digital path so a woman can't find you. And now that I have Willow, I won't be needing that info."

"We'll all join you for a drink or two." Jake shot each of them a look, his gaze lingering on Travis.

They got the message. The next day might be rough on one of their own. A drink or two in support was necessary.

"But we can't stay long," Jake added. "We'll have to be up early."

"Why are you even interested in Kieran's niece?" Tony yanked the door to the showers open. The men filtered past him. "She's a bit brash. And did you see that shirt she was wearing? To a memorial?"

Ryan shrugged. "I saw the way she filled it out. She was rocking the geek chic look. I've never done a nerdy girl before. I didn't realize they could be so hot."

"She just lost her uncle, asshole," Chris reminded him good-naturedly.

"An uncle who wanted a nice Irish boy like myself for his favorite niece." Ryan opened his locker and pulled out a bottle of body wash. "It's practically my duty to show her a good time. You know, cheer her up."

"Yeah, drop your pants and she'll have a good laugh." Chris ducked as the body wash flew past his head.

Tony slammed his own locker door shut. Ryan's jokes were more irritating than usual. Probably because Tony had just ended another failed relationship. He wished he could be as carefree as Ryan. But when Chris's, Travis's, and Jake's women showed at the *Ginger* tonight, like they probably would, he'd feel that familiar pang. The one that told him he was missing out.

No, Melissa might not have been the one for him, but he still knew what he wanted.

And he wasn't going to find it at *The Limber Ginger*.

Tony's phone rang. He opened his locker and pulled it out.

"Is it Melissa calling for a second chance?" Chris asked, a shit-eating grin on his face.

Ryan leaned over and looked at the phone's screen. "Naw. It's the only woman Viper here really loves."

Tony elbowed his out of the way and went to the corner of the locker room. He leaned against the wall as he answered the video call request. "Eloise. How are you doing today, lovely lady?"

"Hi dear, I wanted to ask you..." The older woman pushed her tortoise-shell glasses up her nose and squinted. "Anthony Garcia, did you answer my call in the bathroom?" She stared disapprovingly at his bare chest.

He bit back his grin. Anything he knew about manners, Eloise had taught him. And he lived in dread of ever truly disappointing this woman who had become a surrogate mother to him when he'd needed one most.

Didn't mean he didn't like to ruffle her feathers every now and then. "Don't worry, Elle. I still have my shorts on. I wouldn't answer your call completely nude."

"Well, that young man behind you doesn't have the same consideration."

Tony smothered an oath as he spun to put his back to the wall. Luckily it hadn't been one of his squad to photobomb his call buck naked. Elle had met his friends. She wouldn't be able to look them in the eye without blushing if she'd gotten a look at all their goods.

"Sorry about that." He cleared his throat. "What were you going to ask me?"

Elle sniffed, but there was a twinkle in her eye she couldn't quite hide. "Yes. Well, last time you visited, when we were playing Bingo, you were talking to Fred Sampson. Do you remember Fred?"

"I remember Fred." Fred was a player. He'd already 'dated' half the female population at Eloise's senior living home, and he'd had his eye on Eloise. Tony didn't much care for Fred.

"Well, Fred said that you told him about an author you like. Correga? Cornea?" She toyed with the pearls around her throat.

"Correia. I'll text you his info. Why?"

She patted her steel-gray hair. "Fred's birthday is coming up. He sounded interested in the man's books. I think I'll get him one."

Travis came out of the showers. He twirled a towel up tight and snapped it at Tony's abdomen.

Tony knocked it away, scowling. "Sorry, Elle. My friends are morons. I don't think you need to be getting this Fred anything. He's just a—"

"He's just a nice man who's showing a little interest in me."

"But, Elle, he's a—"

"And when are you going to show some interest in a woman of your own? Enough about my social life. I want to hear about yours." She dipped her chin and peered at him over her glasses.

Travis snorted. "I think Aunt Eloise is getting more action than you are."

Tony hooked his foot behind Travis's ankle and swiped it out from under him. He ignored his friend's pained yelp when he hit the tiled floor. "My social life is fine, Elle."

"Then when are you going to bring a nice girl up to meet me? You know Rosie has a granddaughter—"

"I have to go," Tony said loudly. His friends were getting much too good of a show out of this. "I'll send that author's info to you. Love you, Elle."

"I love you, too. Come visit soon." She blew him a kiss as he disconnected.

Ryan pulled on a pair of khakis. "So, this Rosie's granddaughter—"

Tony took off his shorts and stomped into the showers, ending that conversation. After he put in some time at the *Ginger* tonight, maybe he'd head to that wine bar on 3rd. He'd met Melissa there, after all. And she'd been great. They just hadn't quite clicked. But soon he'd meet the right woman. A class act who also turned his gears.

A woman he'd be proud to take home to Eloise.

And he wasn't going to settle for anything less.

Chapter Six

"You just aim and push the button." Karen held up the small, red tube, mimicking pressing the top button. "It says it has a range of fifteen feet, but I've never tested it."

Bridget wrapped her hand around the pepper spray. "What about you? I don't want to take your only means of self-defense." She stepped back, letting the bartender bustle past.

They were standing behind the bar at *The Limber Ginger*. The place was hopping for a Wednesday night, the laughter and chatter at an abnormally loud buzz. Bridget didn't know what had brought the crowds in, but she wasn't going to complain.

The assistant manager pulled another tube from the pocket of her wide linen slacks. "My brother works at a sporting goods store. I have enough pepper spray to make the whole city cry." She cocked her head. "Are you sure your ex is still in California?"

"Positive." Bridget still had friends at her old company. Kevin had been in the office when they'd left at five-thirty last night and shown up bright and early this morning. Apparently he'd been putting in a lot of long hours since she'd left. With lots of closed-door meetings and raised voices coming from behind those closed doors.

Bridget still didn't know exactly what kind of tight spot Kevin and his father had put themselves in, but she hoped they had a hell of a time pulling themselves out.

"And you're sure the guy was real?" Karen's smile took any bite out of the words. "He wasn't another ghost like you had at your house?"

Bridget never should have told her manager about that scare. "Positive," she bit out. "That was probably just my tired eyes playing tricks on me and a very large raccoon on the porch. This was definitely a man."

"But are you sure it was a creep and not just some poor homeless guy you pelted with trash?"

"My instincts said he was dangerous." At this point, Bridget didn't know which scenario she preferred. That the guy had been dangerous so her actions were justified, or that she was mistaken and there wasn't a dangerous guy who liked to lurk outside her bar.

Karen nodded. "It's always best to follow your instincts."

Bridget slid the pepper spray into its case and shoved it the back pocket of her jeans. "I believe that, too." So why hadn't she followed her instincts with Kevin? Looking back, she knew there was a point when she'd felt something was off. Had she just been too comfortable to break it off? Too scared of change? Was it inertia that had kept her in a pointless relationship?

She pushed away those thoughts. She was out of it now, and navel-gazing did no one any good. She stepped toward the brunette waiting on the other side of the bar. "What can I get for you?"

"We're hoping to get three orders of your spinach artichoke dip," the woman said. She was about Bridget's age, but had the tall, athletic build that Bridget sorely lacked. She pointed to a corner table surrounded by the military guys Bridget had met at the memorial. Two of them had women cuddled up next to them. "I'm with those monsters in the back, and those other two ladies and I form our own little club. The wrong place, wrong time club. Sounds like you could be a member." Her eyes twinkled. "Sorry, I couldn't help but overhear your conversation."

Bridget's gaze caught on a pair of dark chocolate eyes at the table. Familiar eyes. She blinked and looked back at the woman. "I'm surprised you could overhear anything in this mad house."

The brunette stretched out her hand. "I'm Samantha. Sam. I'm sorry, I got to your uncle's memorial late and didn't have a chance to meet you then."

"Bridget." They shook. "Which one is yours?" Bridget asked with a nod toward the table.

"The one who looks like Superman." Sam sighed, a bit dreamily.

Bridget forced her eyes to remain unrolled. Just because her own relationship with love had bitten the dust didn't mean other people couldn't enjoy it. She eyed the table again. All the men could qualify as superheroes with their ripped muscles and handsome faces, but there was one with thick, black hair whose face did resemble that actor's. Lucky girl.

"But don't," Sam said, her face going stern, "tell him I said that. He's already got an ego the size of an air craft carrier."

"Gotcha." She held up a finger and turned to Karen. "Go home, your shift's over. Get Marcus to walk you to your car."

"I don't need him—"

"Please." Kieran would have been the first to insist that the staff be looked after. "For me."

"Fine." Karen shook her head. "I'll put in Sam's order before I leave. See you tomorrow."

"Is there a problem?" Sam asked. "Pepper spray. Getting walked to her car. What happened?"

"Probably nothing. Just a creepy guy hanging around in the alley yesterday." Bridget pressed against the bar to let the bartender slide past. "While you're waiting for the food, can I get you guys anything else to drink?"

"We all have to work tomorrow, so maybe just some bottled water?"

Bridget filled a tray with bottles from the fridge under the bar, added a glass full of lime wedges, and followed Sam to her table. She dodged a chair that backed into her path, stepped over the leg of a man crooning a love song with his friend, and pivoted around a waitress.

Waiting tables she could do. This felt familiar. Easy. Managing all the people in here was another story. She hadn't wanted to let Karen go. Karen knew what she was doing. But Bridget needed to pull on her big girl pants and figure her new job out.

"Here you go." She started placing the bottles down in front of the crowd, circling the table as she did so. As she leant over Tony's shoulder she caught a whiff of his cologne. It smelled expensive, exotic, and all together yummy. She quickly straightened. "If anyone wants anything besides bubbly water, let me know."

"We're good." A blond man with All-American good looks stood and pulled out a vacant chair next to him. Ryan something, if she remembered correctly. "Join us? We didn't get much of a chance to talk at Kieran's memorial. I'd like to get to know the niece he wanted to set me up with." He shot her a devastating smile, one she was sure set women's knees to jelly.

Since she knew his efforts could have happily been directed at any other single woman in the bar, her knees only felt the slightest loosening. She sat anyway. Karen said she had to work on her customer relationship skills, and she might as well start now.

"My uncle must have thought highly of you." She pushed a strand of apricot hair behind her ear. "The summer I stayed with him, he never thought anyone was good enough." She swallowed, her throat thick. That had been a good summer, even with her burly uncle scaring away any boy that came sniffing around.

"It was the name." Travis (*his* name she remembered) rested his forearms on the back of the chair he straddled. "Ryan Kelly. A good Irish name. Then Kieran got to know Hawk, and mentions of his 'darling niece' dried up."

"Hawk?" she asked.

"His call sign." Travis shrugged. "We all have one. Even young Chris here finally got his cherry popped and got one."

The man in question, the one who looked like Superman, threw a balled-up napkin at his friend.

A woman with pin-up good looks and dark curly hair leaned forward. "It's confusing at first, all the names thrown around, but you get used to it. And if you don't remember us from the memorial, I'm Willow and this"—she pointed to a beauty with pale blonde hair—"is Caroline."

"Of course I remember." She totally hadn't. "Nice to see you again."

Sam leaned against Chris, using his body as a backrest. "Now tell us why you're carrying pepper spray and Karen needs to get walked to her car. Did you get robbed?"

The men's postures didn't change, but they seemed to get bigger somehow. "Problems?" The man she'd been introduced to as Jake asked.

"Probably nothing. Just a creepy guy out in the alley yesterday." She waved her hand airily. She tried to make her mood match her actions. She probably had overreacted. It was probably just some homeless dude that she'd scared as much as he had her.

"Creepy how?" The voice was low. Smooth. And demanded that she turn and look at the one man whose gaze she'd avoided since sitting down.

Tony Garcia was wearing slacks and a lightweight blue sweater that looked great against his skin. An artist couldn't have done a better job than that sweater in showcasing his wide shoulders or the tan, thick column of his throat.

She hadn't known necks could be sexy.

She pushed away that irrelevant thought. "I came upon some guy by the dumpster when I was taking the trash out. He didn't say anything, didn't threaten me, but he was just...."

"Creepy." Willow nodded.

"What happened?" Sam asked impatiently.

"Nothing." Bridget shifted back in her chair, and the pepper spray pressed against her behind. "He took a step toward me, I threw a bag of garbage at his head, and I high-tailed it back into the bar. When Marcus our cook went to look, he was gone." Each time she retold it, her worries sounded even sillier. But there had been that feeling of menace. Like he'd been waiting for her.

"Did you recognize him?" Chris asked.

"No. He was wearing a ball cap pulled low and the collar of his coat covered half his face."

"Like he was trying not to be seen." Tony's voice held an edge.

Bridget lifted one shoulder. "I assumed crazy or drug use."

Tony sighed. "With this kind of bar, I guess you have to expect that sort of thing."

"This kind of bar?" She kept her voice pleasant, but every vertebrae in her spine rolled straight.

"Viper here is more of a wine bar kind of guy." Travis snorted. "He's Navy," he added, as though that explained it.

"I'm sure even the alleys behind wine bars have their share of problems." Bridget gazed around Kieran's bar. Hers now. It was loud. Rowdy. Cheerful. And she loved it. "My customers are hard-working and need a place to blow off steam. I'm happy to provide it."

A woman in a white tank top and sky-high heels climbed onto her chair and started singing karaoke style. Unfortunately, the lyrics she belted out didn't match the song that was playing.

Tony arched a dark eyebrow.

"Real salt-of-the-earth kind of people." Her cheeks were starting to strain with her forced smile.

A body knocked into her chair, jerking her forward. Ryan jumped up with a scowl and pulled a man in jeans and a Panthers' jersey back several steps. When he released his hold on the man's collar, the guy's knees sagged.

With an eyeroll, Ryan steadied him.

"Hey." The man pointed at Bridget with his beer mug, his lager sloshing dangerously near the rim. "Kieran's daughter."

"Niece," she corrected.

The man blinked. Staggered. "Kieran's kid. Whatever. The Limbo...Limber Ginger. That named after you?"

Bridget twisted in her seat to face him. She calculated how close to puking the guy was and if she needed to hurry him out of here. She pressed her lips together. He probably had another half hour before he got in the danger zone, but he was being cut off as of now. "Nope. It was named after my Mom."

The man leered. He probably thought it was a smile that would charm the pants off a lady. "You limber too?" He scanned her body. "I've got this book. And it's got these positions. And—"

"Okay, that's enough." Ryan herded him back toward his own table.

"But it's even got pictures...." His voice was drowned out in the crowd.

When Bridget turned back, Tony was smirking. "Salt of the earth?"

She raised her hands, palms up. "Some of them are salti-er than others."

Sam burst out laughing. "I guess being around a lot of drinking you can't take offense to comments like those."

"I'm Irish." Bridget reached for Ryan's unopened bottle of water. She'd get him another. "We don't get offended. And my mom was limber. She was a gymnast until she got too tall for the sport."

Patty hurried up, her tray tucked under one arm. An anxious look covered her pretty face, but then, the woman was always anxious. She'd almost fainted when a kid had shot her with some silly string. Silly string, for Christ's sake.

"What's up?" Bridget asked. Her uncle must have kept Patty on for a reason. If he could be patient, so could she.

"Um." Patty twisted the end of her dark ponytail around her finger. "We might have a problem."

Bridget rolled her neck. With Patty a problem could be anything from them running low on their local ale to Patty being scheduled to work on another moving day, she thought snidely. Then had to eat her words. Or thoughts, as the case may be. Because there, where Patty was point-ing, in the center of the *Ginger*, a full-on brawl was break-ing out.

Bridget jumped up. "Oh, shit."

"Swear jar," the waitress reminded her.

Bridget ignored her and elbowed her way forward, into the melee. She had a feeling by the end of the night, that swear jar was going to be overflowing.

Chapter Seven

THE ELBOW OF THE woman in the towering heels caught Tony in the chin. Things went downhill from there.

He grabbed the arm of the drunk throwing the slowest haymaker of all time and twisted it behind the man's back. "Easy there. Time to call it a night."

He didn't catch the man's response. A chair flew past his head, and he ducked just in time. A streak of red hair and an avalanche of cursing that would make a sailor applaud caught his attention just before the bar's owner ducked beneath a table and scuttled out of sight.

"This isn't our problem." Ryan appeared at his elbow. "I think we should— Watch out!" He shoved Tony's side, causing him to stumble a step forward. A red-feathered dart flew past his temple, missing him by inches.

A pained squawk told him some other poor sucker hadn't been as lucky.

Jake pushed through the throng. "Get the waitstaff safely behind the bar. I've already called the police."

Tony and Ryan nodded and headed in different directions. Tony pushed his way toward the center of the melee, dodging drunken combatants and the odd flying beer mug. He found Bridget trying to herd one belligerent toward the exit using a wooden chair the way a lion tamer might poke at an annoyed large cat.

The drunk it was directed at merely looked confused.

"Come on." Tony tugged the chair from her hands and set it down.

She picked it back up. "Go outside. I'll handle this."

The drunk, tired of being poked at, brought his thick hand down, swatting the chair to the floor. "Where's Beezur? Wha' didya do to Beezur?"

"He's outside waiting for you." Bridget planted her hands on her hips. "Stop keeping him waiting. Go on."

"'Kay." The man lumbered toward the door.

Bridget nodded and turned to a pair of men wrestling on the ground.

"No." Tony grabbed her wrist. "Leave them for the police."

"It's my bar they're busting up. I'm—"

A man staggered into them, a woman clinging to his back, pulling his long, gray ponytail. Bridget reached for the woman and got the heel of a boot planted into her gut. She doubled over, another foul word leaving her pretty lips, and suddenly, Tony had enough.

"Right." He swept the man's leg, sending him and the woman crashing to the floor. With one step and a quick bend at his waist, he tossed Bridget up onto his shoulder and strode to her office. He slammed the door shut behind him before depositing her on her feet.

She gaped up at him. "What the hell? You can't just go around tossing people up on your shoulder and dragging them about?"

"Apparently I can," he said mildly.

She narrowed her eyes, her face flushing. "Don't get cute with me. You know what I mean. You had no right. Now if you'll excuse me, there's a bar brawl I need to break up." She stomped toward the door.

Tony leaned back against it, crossing one ankle over the other. "You, of all people, are not going to stop a fight."

She grabbed the knob, her arm brushing his hip, and yanked. The door didn't move. She pressed her foot to the wall beside the door and tried again.

Tony's lips quirked. She was tenacious. He'd give her that.

"What do you mean, me of all people?" She gave up her attacks on the door and started a more direct assault. She grabbed his arm and tried prying him away from the exit.

"You're what, five feet tall?" He thought about moving forward an inch, letting her feel that she was having some success, but decided it would be better if she realized the futility of her actions sooner rather than later.

She paused long enough to give him an outraged glare. "I'm five foot three." She switched from pulling on him to pushing. Her fingers pressed into his side. Her breast pushed against his arm.

The base of his spine tingled. Her tee shirt tonight showed a picture of a dragon lifting a barbell with the words "Do you even Crit?" written above and below it. He had no idea what it meant, but he had to admit the dragon stretched across her curves quite nicely. With each attempt to push him aside on her part, the fabric slackened then grew taut as she rubbed against him.

He dragged his gaze away. "Those extra three inches won't help you against angry drunks."

"My staff—"

"The other guys are looking out for them." He knew Jake and the others wouldn't let any of the waitresses get hurt. Although he suspected that the employees of the *Ginger* were smart enough to get the heck out of Dodge when the fists started flying. Too bad the owner wasn't as sensible.

"You wouldn't have dragged my uncle back here." She finally gave in and stepped back, her chest heaving with her exertion.

A part of Tony was disappointed. "Kieran was built like a grizzly bear. And it's because of him that I pulled you out of there."

"Carried me out," she muttered. "How long are you going to keep me back here? This is false imprisonment, by the way."

"Until the cops come and break the fights up." He looked at the piles of papers stacked all over the small room. It was safer than looking at her. Anger had only made her prettier. He wondered what she'd look like out of those absurd tee shirts, in a nice skirt and some heels. She'd probably clean up nice.

She'd look best in nothing at all.

He cleared his throat. "I guess you have to expect this sort of thing here. You might want to think about hiring a bouncer."

"I can't even afford cameras, much less a bouncer. And what do you mean, 'This sort of thing here.'" Bridget seemed overly fond of repeating his words back to him. "You mean a place with cheap beer and cheaper people?"

Heat flushed through his body. "I didn't say that. And cameras aren't that expensive." They would be a good investment for a place like this. At least to give to the police as evidence when brawls broke out.

"But you meant it." She pushed a jar of pens out of the way and plopped her rear end on her desk. "You're a snob."

"I am not." He pushed away from the door. Just because he liked nice things didn't mean he looked down on anyone else. "My mom used to wait tables in a place a hell of a lot worse than this."

"Worse than this? The *Ginger* isn't a dive bar. We get families in here for dinner." She gripped the edge of the desk and leaned forward. "Why do you even bother coming here if you want high end wine and jazz music?"

"I hate jazz music and I come here because my squad does," he growled. "Just because I prefer going places where my shoes don't stick to the floor doesn't make me a snob." Nor did the fact that he liked his women in heels and pearls instead of jeans and sneakers. A man couldn't control whom he was attracted to.

The sound of sirens reached them. The office was next to the parking lot, and the faint blue light from a squad car flickered through the window.

Bridget hopped off the desk. "Cops are here. Am I allowed to go out now or do I need to pay some sort of toll to my jailor?" She gave him a smile that was all teeth.

Tony counted to ten. Then counted again. This was Kieran's niece. A man he'd respected and who'd been nothing but kind to him and his friends. He could take some attitude if it meant Kieran's niece was unharmed.

He opened the door and made sure there were no more sounds of battle before stepping aside. "Do me a favor. Next time fists start flying, don't try to break up the fight yourself."

"Sure." She sounded about as sincere as Ryan did when he promised to call a woman the next day. She brushed past him, the scent of something sweet and floral teasing his nose.

He padded after her. The bar didn't look as bad as he'd feared. Some broken glasses. One overturned table. A shirt without its owner laying crumpled in the middle of the floor. Several drunks in zip ties were being led out of the bar, but it didn't look like anyone was badly hurt. He nodded to Jake who pressed a pack of ice to his eye. The rest of the guys had minor scratches and bruises.

Bridget sighed. "Clean up is going to suck tonight."

"There is a lot of spilled beer," he agreed.

She shot him a side-long glance. "And I wouldn't want anyone's shoes to stick to the floor."

"I appreciate it." The bartender pointed one of the cops in their direction. Tony knew the police would want to speak to the owner privately, but he was oddly reluctant to leave her.

"Well, it could have been worse." She shoved her hands in the back pockets of her jeans and surveyed the damage.

He snorted. "Could have been better, too."

Her shoulders slumped. "A lot of things could be better."

Tony scratched his chest. Her problems weren't his business. He shouldn't care. He didn't. "What can I do?" he found himself asking.

She blew out a breath. "Nothing. My uncle created a great bar"—she shot him a defiant glare, almost inviting him to debate that conclusion—"but he let a lot of things slide," she continued. "Like painting, replacing some dry rot, installing security cameras." She twisted her mouth wryly. "But it's nothing I can't handle."

She strode away to meet the approaching cop.

Tony's gaze slipped to her pert backside before snapping up. This was Kieran's niece. He shouldn't ogle her. He wasn't even attracted to her, for God's sake. She wasn't his type.

And she was wrong. There was something he could do to help her. And he wanted to help her.

For Kieran's sake.

Chapter Eight

THEIR TEAM CHIEF, MASTER Sergeant Jonathan Price, bounced his pen up and down on the table before him. He sat ramrod-straight next to Jake, with the rest of Alpha squad flanking them on either side. "My squad was concerned for the safety of the civilians in the establishment and stepped in to act. They will always act in the manner that they believe will result in the lowest amount of civilian casualties. Just as they did with the actions this inquiry is concerned about."

One of the four members leading the inquiry leaned forward, resting her hands on the table opposite from the squad. This session was supposed to be informal, an information gathering, but it felt like they were already on trial. "Or, the fact that your men got into a bar fight last night demonstrates their lack of discipline. We're here to assess the decision-making capabilities of Alpha squad, and right now, it doesn't look good." She swept her hand out, indicating the bruises and scratches on the squad member's faces.

Tony and his friends were in uniform, every edge sharply pressed, but the presentation of military readiness was somewhat diminished with Jake's black eye, Ryan's puffy lip, and the fact that Travis and Chris looked like they'd both taken chairs to the faces. The injuries were all superficial, but on a day when they needed to look their most responsible, well, it didn't look great.

The captain in front of them gathered his papers. "We'll examine your most recent mission statements and let you know what we decide. In the meantime, you're off rotation until this after-action review is concluded. Delta will take your next operation."

"Sir," Price began.

"Dismissed." The captain and the three other investigators stood and filed from the room. Price and the squad stood at attention until the door closed behind them.

Tony rolled his shoulders. "I'd like to know what they would have done if they were at the *Ginger* last night. Hid under their tables?"

Price shoveled some documents into his briefcase. "Perhaps, when they noticed the night was getting a bit rowdy, they would have left before any trouble started." He turned to Jake. "This was not a good look for your men."

"Understood." Even with a swollen eye, Jake managed to look stoic and commanding. "But regardless of whether we made a mistake helping last night, Kowalski's shot was good. It was on my authority that he took it. His military career won't be harmed because of it."

Price ran a hand over his tight, black curls. "There's the right way to do something, the wrong way, and then there's the military way. In a perfect world, you'd be right. I hope you're right. Enjoy your time off men." He nodded at them then strode from the room.

Travis kicked his chair, sending it skidding across the room. "You didn't give me the order to shoot, Psych. There wasn't time. If they find it was a bad shoot, you're not going to fall on your sword."

Jake gripped his shoulder. "I'm the Element Leader of Alpha squad. It was under my authority. And they're going to see that it was justified."

Ryan picked up the chair and returned it to its spot. "You still have a lot of confidence in the military's ability to make the right decision." They filed out and headed to the gym to change.

"You don't?" Chris rubbed at a scratch that bisected his cheek.

Ryan snorted. "It's my home. I'll ride or die for the Marines. But you gotta admit, we're not the fighting force we once were. Standards are lowered every day. The brass cares more about how the military looks and less about it being the most deadly fighting force on the planet. They probably think we should have held the terrorist's hand and counseled him on the error of his mean ways rather than take him down."

Tony blinked at the disgust in his friend's voice as he changed clothes. It wasn't uncommon to hear these complaints from those serving, but it was the first time he'd heard one of his squad members voice them. "But that's not us. That's not the Raiders, or any other special forces team. We're still elite."

"And we will continue to be," Jake added mildly. He grabbed his range bag from his locker. "Now let's go to the range and train."

They filed out after him, each shouldering their own bags. "Blowing shit up does make me feel better." Travis slapped a ball cap on his head when they were outside.

Jake scanned the area before slipping his sunglasses on. He muttered something under his breath.

"Something wrong?" Tony asked him.

"Can't get rid of this feeling." Jake followed the path toward the range. "Something bad's coming. We should go on the next op, not Delta. They won't have much down time between missions."

"We don't get that a lot of times either." Chris rolled his shoulders. "It's the job."

Jake grunted.

Uneasiness swirled through Tony's gut. Jake's "feelings" were usually prophetic. Was Travis facing a court-martial for the shot he'd taken? Was that what Jake's gut was telling him? Taking out the terrorist hadn't been a part of their carefully planned operation, but it had been justified. And there was no way Tony was going to let his brother-in-arms face the heat alone.

"It's also the job to have each other's backs." Ryan elbowed Tony. "Why is your face still pretty? Were *you* hiding under a table while the rest of us got our hands dirty?"

"I was preventing a crazy midget from getting hurt." Tony huffed. "Can you believe that Bridget wanted to break up the fight herself? She refused to leave, so I took her to the back office."

"And did what with her there?" Travis waggled his eyebrows.

"Argued mostly." Tony frowned. "You guys aren't suggesting that I'm interested in Kieran's niece, are you? The ball-buster in weird T-shirts and sneakers? You do know me, right?"

"Cute is cute." Chris nodded to a newbie who tripped over his feet to salute them. "Is there going to be a competition between you and Ryan over who lands the saucy barkeep? 'Cause that could be entertaining."

Ryan shrugged. "Naw, she's all his. I never got the look from Bridget. You know, the one that said she'd be down for a little rough and tumble. Tony can take his shot."

Tony shoved through the gate that led to the range. "I don't want a shot. I was just watching out for Kieran's niece like he would have wanted. Same reason I'm going to help her paint the *Ginger*."

All the guys stopped as one, causing the range master to glance their way.

"What?" Damn, hadn't he mentioned his plans to the guys earlier? The way they were acting, he should have kept his mouth shut. "Bridget's struggling, and Kieran would have wanted us to help."

There was a moment of silence. "So when are we meeting over there to paint?" Jake finally asked.

"I didn't mean you guys had to...."

Travis let out an obnoxious hoot. "So our help isn't wanted, but Kieran wanted *you* to give his lovely niece a hand."

The back of Tony's neck went hot. "That's not what I meant." What was wrong with his friends? Couldn't a guy try to do something nice without it meaning something more?

"Oh, we're going to help," Chris said. He picked up a stack of targets. "Not only because we now have some time on our hands, but because I wouldn't miss seeing you trying *not* to flirt with the woman you're pretending you're not interested in."

Tony gritted his teeth. "I'm not interested in her."

Travis slapped him on the back. "Then it shouldn't be a problem that we join you at the bar. You're not interested, so there's no way we'd be messing with your game. Right?"

Tony's gaze slid away from Jake's arched eyebrow. From the mocking grins on the other assholes' faces. "Right," he bit out. He took his Glock 19 from his bag and slid on his eye and ear protection. Maybe he should keep his hearing protector on full-time so he wouldn't have to listen to his so-called friends.

Jake slid an uneasy glance up and down the range before stepping up to his own stall.

Tony loaded a magazine. He wasn't concerned about Jake's latest 'bad feeling,' anymore. He knew what the premonition was about.

Tony was going to murder all his squad mates if they joked about his supposed attraction to Bridget one more time. And he'd do it with a smile.

Chapter Nine

"I CAN'T BELIEVE I let you talk me into this." Bridget slapped at the jab Sam sent her way. Then shrieked and ducked when the woman followed it up with a right hook.

"Yeah." Sam cocked her head, her chestnut ponytail slipping over her shoulder. "I really thought you'd be better at this for some reason."

They were at a martial arts studio near the center of town that Sam attended. Over drinks with the girlfriends of Tony's friends, Bridget had learned that Tony and the others weren't just military but special forces. Marine Raiders. She'd also learned that Tony was the Navy corpsman of the squad and supposedly a very sweet guy, although Bridget had seen little evidence to support that theory so far. She'd met Willow's adorable daughter, Matilda, who'd seemed thrilled to have a Shirley Temple with the girls. She'd also learned that Sam had just earned her orange belt in Hapkido.

Somehow, between the beer and the cheesecake, Bridget had agreed to try out the dojo with Sam. A decision she was now regretting.

"I've never been what you'd call athletic," Bridget admitted. Much to her family's dismay. "The only thing I can sort of do without tripping over my own feet is medieval swordplay. I used to participate in reenactments at the local Ren Faire."

Sam blinked.

"It's a thing," Bridget said defensively. The sword was her weapon of choice when she played role playing games so it had only seemed logical to try it in real life, as well. And she'd had a surprising aptitude for it. "Unfortunately, there's no Olympic sport for historical melee weapons."

Sam slid another punch toward her, moving slowly enough so Bridget could parry it. "Why would you want there to be an Olympic sport?"

Bridget shrugged. "The Olympics are a big part of my family's life."

"Wait." Sam easily knocked Bridget's hand down and stepped inside with an elbow to her chest. "Your brother's not the swimmer Sean Sullivan, is he?"

"Yep." Bridget watched the pair of brown belts next to them flawlessly execute the move, following up the elbow to the chest with a dropping technique that ended with one man flat on his back. Bridget hadn't gotten past the parry and elbow yet.

"That's amazing," Sam said. "And your parents...?"

"Both Olympians, too. That's actually where they met. My mom was a triathlete and my dad was in track and field. Still coaches it actually." And then there was Bridget. A full foot shorter than her father and brother, seven inches shorter than her mom, and with a higher body fat percentage than probably all three of them combined. Family photos had never been fun for her.

Maybe that's why she'd been so pissy with Tony when he'd carried her to the office. She was used to being manhandled by people twice her size, and she hated it. Her brother thought it was great fun to mess with his 'shrimp' of a sister.

Something twisted low in her belly. Being tossed over Tony's shoulder was a very different experience than when her brother did it. Still annoying, but kind of hot, too. Not that she'd ever admit that to the man.

The instructor, a man in his mid-fifties named John, called everyone over to watch while he demonstrated a new move. It started with the same jab/cross combination, then he dropped to one knee, wrapped an arm around his opponent's waist, and somersaulted, bringing his attacker tumbling down.

A blue belt asked a question about breaking your attacker's neck with that take-down, and Bridget cupped her own neck protectively. Coming to this class really, *really* hadn't been a good idea.

"That's why we go slowly in this class and practice falling," John explained, rolling to his feet. He ran a hand over his bald pate. "If the guy attacking you doesn't know how to fall and doesn't tuck his head, then yeah, bad things can happen. Gives you more time to get away. Besides, if someone comes at you, don't cry over what they get. I just tell them, not my fault your dead."

Sam snorted, then dragged Bridget back to their spot on the mat. "Come on. We'll go really slowly."

Bridget fumbled through the moves. She had Karen's pepper spray. Surely that was good enough for self-defense. She couldn't imagine herself, not in a million years, ever taking someone down like this in real life.

The instructor came up to them and adjusted something in Sam's positioning. He watched as Sam fed Bridget a punch.

"My grandmother could block a punch faster than that." John crossed his arms. "Do you like your partner?" he asked Sam.

"Well, we don't know each other all that well," Sam said, shrugging, "but sure."

"Thanks," Bridget said, sarcastic.

"If you like her, then don't go so easy," he said. "A bad guy sure won't. Give her around seventy percent of your real punch."

Well, that made sense. If that guy in the alley had come at her, he sure wouldn't have been slow-rolling his punches. He would have—

Bridget didn't see it coming until it was too late. Her hand jerked up to parry, but Sam's jab was already landing. The blow caught her on her right cheek, snapping her head back with the impact.

Bridget blinked, the dojo around her not quite in focus. Feeling like standing was just too much effort at this point, she let her legs crumple until she sat cross-legged on the mat, staying well out of reach of anyone else's arms.

Bridget jerked to a stop in the doorway of *The Limber Ginger*. It was Monday, the day they were closed, which meant the place should have been empty, but men in various stages of undress were scattered around the bar, paint brushes in hand.

Hot men.

Travis had opted for the full painter's get-up, complete with overalls and a paint-smeared cap. Chris and Jake wore shorts and tees, their biceps rippling as they rolled paint onto the far wall. Ryan wore cargo shorts and nothing else, flecks of the brown paint sticking to the firm flesh of his back.

And Tony.... Well, Tony stood in the middle of the dining area, denim jeans molding around his taut lower body, his own shirt in his hand as he scraped at a mark on the blue fabric with his thumbnail. The firm expanse of his chest was lightly furred, and his pec muscles twitched with each angry swipe of his thumb. His shoulders, which had always seemed broad, looked as wide as the Atlantic without a shirt to cover them.

Bridget's tongue seemed to fill her mouth. The man should never wear clothes. She could only imagine what a sight he'd be without his pants.

He looked up, and she darted her glance away, hoping it wasn't obvious she'd been ogling. "What are you guys doing?" She directed her question to Jake. He was handsome, no doubt, but safer to look at.

Karen hurried around the bar, a bucket in hand. "We've got free labor for the afternoon. Well, I did promise them dinner as thank-you's, but you can't beat that deal."

"Yes, but why?" Bridget stepped fully inside, letting the door swing shut behind her. The rectangle of sunlight that had backlit her faded to nothing.

"Whoa." Karen placed the bucket of soapy water on the floor and examined her. "A ghost didn't do that."

Bridget pressed a finger to her eye. She'd hoped the bruise hadn't been too obvious.

Tony dropped his shirt and strode toward her. "What happened?" His normally smooth voice was low and rough.

Her eyes skittered over his chest, across the two-inch scar that crossed his collar bone, and settled somewhere over his shoulder. She pointed at Chris. "His girlfriend punched me."

"What?" A furrow creased Tony's forehead as Chris sighed. Tony placed two fingers under her chin and tilted her face to the light. His thumb gently brushed along her jaw bone as he examined her eye.

"I was supposed to duck," she explained, her heart jumping about like a child on a sugar high. Just because the most beautiful man she'd ever known was touching her, was close enough to kiss, was no reason to act like a moron. "Or was it parry? Anyway, my mind blanked and I did neither. Hence, the eye." At Tony's continued confused look, "She took me to a martial arts class."

Chris wiped his brow with the hem of his shirt. "She loves that class. She can get a little...exuberant when she's training." The edge of his mouth curled up. "I train with her at home as much as I can."

"There's a reason Caroline only went with her to that class once." Jake frowned and turned to Karen. "Did you say 'ghost'?"

"She was joking." Bridget said the words so quickly they tumbled over one another. Her cheeks heated as she pulled back from Tony's hold. "There's no ghost."

"There were weird noises and lights at Kieran's house the other night." Karen stretched her back. "We decided it was a really big raccoon."

Marcus plodded in from the back, an extension ladder under one arm. "I told you I got a cousin who can trap that for you if you want. Cleetus even removes unwanted skunks, but he chargers extra for them."

"The house is out in the country. Wild animals are part of the deal." She took her first real look at the progress the men had made. Most of the walls were finished, just waiting to dry before they could remove the blue painter's tape that edged the trim. Flakes of old paint dusted the floor, but a good sweep and mop and the place would look like new. It was amazing what a coat of paint could do.

She stepped forward and gave the room a slow 360 degree appraisal. "You guys have done amazing work. I can't thank you enough."

Marcus snorted. "You think these jarheads know how to paint? I had to show 'em the right end of the brush to hold." He turned, moving for the back wall, and the end of the ladder swung at Bridget.

Before she could jump back, strong arms wrapped around her waist and pulled her away.

She knew whose chest her back was pressed against. Whose bare, muscled chest. He'd never picked up his shirt. She told her body to calm the fuck down. He was just being nice.

She pursed her lips. If she thought a curse word, did she still have to put money in the swear jar?

"Come on." Tony took her hand and tugged her toward the bar. "Let's get some ice on that eye or you'll look like Psych."

They went behind it. Tony found a clean dishtowel, scooped ice from the chest into it, and twisted the towel closed. He handed her the ice pack, which turned out to be a convenient distraction. She was caught completely unawares when he gripped her hips and lifted her onto the bar.

"Hey. Stop manhandling me."

He pulled a penlight from the pocket of his jeans and aimed it at her eyes.

She flinched and turned her head.

"Hold still." He cupped her jaw and held her face steady. "I just want to check that you don't have a concussion."

"Aw, I don't remember Viper checking any of us out after the bar fight." Travis made obnoxious kissing sounds.

Tony's hand tightened on her jaw. "Any dizziness? Nausea?"

"No." She pulled away and glared. There wasn't much heat in it. As much as she hated to admit it, it turned out her body didn't mind being manhandled if the man handling it was over six feet of muscle and determination. "Are you a doctor?"

"The corpsman of the squad."

"Hmph." She cocked her head. She didn't know much about this man other than that he was pushy and liked finer establishments than her bar. But she wanted to. "How did you get the name Viper?"

She didn't think it was possible for a special forces operator to blush, but it was a close thing with Tony.

"Long story," he said.

Ryan strolled up and leaned his elbows on the bar. "It really isn't."

Tony glared at him. "Too long for here."

"I don't know." She narrowed her eyes. "You guys seem to have lots of time on your hands if you can come help me paint. Why are you here exactly?"

Ryan blinked, eyes wide. "Yeah, Viper. Why are we here exactly?"

"Kieran would have wanted us to help," he bit out.

Travis circled behind the bar and grabbed a bottle of water from the mini-fridge. "We do like to be helpful." With a smile that was too innocent by half, he leaned around Tony, handing a bottle to Ryan. He stumbled over nothing and fell against Tony's back, causing him to bump against Bridget. "Shit. Sorry, man."

It was all so silly. The set-up was only too apparent. But as Bridget's legs automatically widened to bracket around Tony's hips, as her palm splayed across his pec and felt the heat underneath her skin, she couldn't find it in herself to be angry with his friends.

"I'm sorry," Tony muttered. His head swung back from glaring at his friend and his gaze locked with hers. He blinked.

There was some surprise in his eyes. A bit of confusion. But the heat was undeniable.

She knew she wasn't his type. Knew he'd probably never looked at a woman like her twice.

She also knew animal attraction when she felt it. It had been something that had been sorely lacking in her past relationship. It went beyond types and preferences.

And she and Tony had it.

Forgetting they were in a public place, surrounded by his friends, she arched her back to get closer. She wanted to show him that even nerds could be sexy. Show him that he didn't have to be confused. He was a man; she was a woman. It didn't have to be more complicated than that.

His mouth was close. The musky scent of his sweat sent a tingle straight down her spine. She rocked closer, feeling his breath on her lips.

"We have to go."

Bridget blinked, trying to place the voice.

Tony stepped back, leaving her cold. "What happened?"

Jake slid his phone into his back pocket. "Redwood just texted. Jakov's father visited the base. Wanted to tell him in person."

"Tell him what?" Ryan straightened from the bar.

"His brother was found murdered this morning."

"Jesus." Chris closed his eyes. "Let's go see if we can help."

"Who?" Bridget asked Tony. Someone they knew had been murdered? Or the brother of someone they knew. She couldn't even imagine.

"A guy from Delta squad, a part of our MSOT." At her look. "Marine Special Operations Team." He strode around the bar and plucked his shirt from the floor. She spun on her butt to face him. "I'm sorry we didn't finish," he began.

She waved her hand. "Go. Thank you all so much for your help, but take care of your friend."

The men nodded goodbye and filed from the bar. It felt like all the energy went with them, leaving the *Ginger* hollowed out.

"Damn." Karen dropped into a chair. "That poor guy's family was probably always worried about when he went on missions. Probably weren't prepared for a son at home getting killed."

"Can you ever really prepare for losing a kid?"

Karen raised one shoulder. "Well, this day sure turned sucky."

And then it got even worse.

Bridget's phone rang. Seeing it was her own brother, she answered with more eagerness than normal. She couldn't imagine losing him. "Hey, Sean. What's up?"

"Thank fuck." He blew out a gusty sigh. "I was scared you were at the house."

"Why?" She slid off the bar. Dread coiled in her belly.

"Just got a call from the city. Kieran's house is on fire."

Chapter Ten

BRIDGET PRESSED THE BOTTLE to her lips, enjoying the bite of the lager as she watched the sun kiss the horizon. The view from Kieran's roof was fantastic. The work she had left to do on it less so.

The thick plastic she'd stapled to the shingles rustled lightly with the breeze. She'd been lucky. The fire had smoked more than burned, catching the eye of the nearest neighbor, and had been quickly put out by the county firefighters. The house wasn't technically in the city limits, and a county firehouse was only three miles away.

She took another pull on the bottle. The chief told her he thought a spark from someone burning trash must have landed on her roof. There was now a roughly three foot charred hole, boarded over with a thin bit of plywood her uncle had in the shed and covered with plastic, but that was the extent of the damage. The hole wasn't even over a room. Not even over the attic. Just led into a weird crawlspace.

Yes, she'd been lucky. So why didn't she feel it?

The lavender sky darkened to amethyst. Bridget finished her drink and gathered her tools. She scuttled to the ladder propped against the eave and twisted her body onto it. The skin on the back of her neck crawled. This was how Uncle Kieran had died. Had there been time for him to be frightened? Had he lain on the floor in pain or died instantly? Her ladder was solidly planted into the ground by the front porch, but her shoulders didn't relax until her sneakers hit the dirt.

Her phone beeped with an incoming text as she put everything away. Kevin. She was tired of his bizarre accusations. Tired of any connection to him at all. She blocked his number, her lips tilting up. He could pester her as much as he wanted and she wouldn't know.

Grabbing some food, she headed to the living room. Instead of continuing to pack up Kieran's things, she plonked down on the couch and reached for her headset and laptop. With a quick message to some friends, she was set up for gaming in less than five minutes.

"Where've you been?" *Elf Lord 888* asked her. "You missed our last game."

"Sorry." She gave a quick run-down of her uncle's death and her move across the country.

"And now you own a tavern?" *One and Only Glorfindel* asked. "Cool."

Bridget started setting up her character. "Yeah, I guess." Cool. Scary as hell. Same thing. She chose a female warrior with a boob-to-waist ratio mere mortals could only dream of, made her a height Bridget could only dream of, and clothed her in samurai armor. Or tried to. A warning popped up:

Your choice might be culturally offensive. Do you want to reconsider?

Bridget pounded the keys on her keyboard a mite too hard. "I just want to steal some gold and kill some orcs. I don't want a side of sensitivity training served along with it."

Elf Lord 888 snorted. "Causing trouble already. You're just pissy because you missed our last game. You know you need this as an outlet. We're cheaper than therapy."

He wasn't wrong. The more battles they won, the lighter Bridget felt. Maybe she should look at her current circumstances as a new quest. A new beginning. She'd suffered a loss, yes, but she'd also been gifted with amazing opportunities. She was a tavern owner, and everyone knew all the best adventures were hatched in taverns. So she'd had a little bar fight. And a fire. A game wasn't fun unless it was a challenge. If life was easy, it would be boring.

Her optimism lasted until lights sparked in the corner of her eye. She jerked her head up. The air near the ceiling seemed to glisten, like fine motes of glitter were floating in the air.

A shiver slid down her spine. "I've gotta go," she whispered to her friends before taking her headset off. That was when she heard it. It was soft, and it had been hidden by the game's music and her friends' chatter. A muffled thump followed by a rasp. Like someone taking a step and dragging something heavy on the floor.

She rose, staring at the ceiling. It could just be a raccoon, lugging something it stole up to her attic. They were sneaky fuckers, no doubt. Maybe there was a raccoon party happening up there. They could be wearing hats for all she knew.

The front porch creaked, and Bridget jumped. There was a rap, another, sharp as gunfire.

She rubbed her palms on the thighs of her jeans. She didn't believe in ghosts. Spooky lights and a surround-sound of weird noises didn't mean anything. There was another rap. A creak, this time on her side porch. She almost didn't hear it over the rush of blood in her ears.

She tiptoed to the hall closet where she'd stashed some of her things and grabbed the hilt of her broadsword. A shadow flickered past the kitchen window. Heart thudding, she crept to the back door. She eased out onto the back porch, grateful that her uncle had kept the hinges on the doors well oiled.

The boards on the side porch creaked. Whatever it was, it was getting closer.

She tightened her grip on the hilt, shifted her weight to prepare for a battle charge, and stared at the corner of the house. No challenges, no fun, right? Her stomach twisted. She was a warrior. She never turned down a quest. Whatever came around that corner, she could handle.

The darkness shifted. A form emerged. And with a cry worthy of Brunhilda, she leveled her sword and charged.

"I am *so* sorry."

Tony grimaced as Bridget apologized for the twentieth time. He grimaced even more when she dumped half a bottle of isopropyl alcohol over the cut on his palm.

Note to self: grabbing the pointy end of a sword wasn't his best idea. Although it was better than being stabbed with it. When he'd seen the hobbit-sized Bridget charging at him carrying a sword almost as tall as she was, he'd been stunned into a moment of immobility. It had cost him.

Not much. Just a slice on his hand that didn't need stitches. But he prayed his squad never learned that Kieran's niece had drawn first blood.

She dabbed around the wound with a folded piece of gauze before pressing it over the cut. "Uh, in all the excitement, I never asked. Why are you here?" She kept her head lowered, her gaze fixed on her task as she taped the makeshift bandage on. She knelt between his legs as he sat on the toilet in her bathroom, her apricot hair piled in a messy bun on the top of her head.

His mind flashed to something completely inappropriate. It was hard not to, seeing their relative positions. His cock twitched. He jerked his hand away, took both of her shoulders, and lifted her as he stood. He set her a respectable distance away. "I'd left my watch at the *Ginger*. When I went back for it, Karen told me that your house was on fire."

She cocked her head, one eyebrow arching. The purple bruises beneath her eye somewhat diminished the haughty look she was going for. They also made him want to do foolish things. Like take her in his arms and press soft kisses to the swollen flesh.

"And so you came running over?" she asked.

"You make it sound as though that's weird." Needing air, he pushed past her and into the much more spacious...bedroom. Damn, that was a big bed. Kieran had been a large man, so it made sense, but.... His gaze flew to Bridget, who'd followed him out. Damn.

"Most people wouldn't have come." She crossed her arms over her T-shirt. The words 'The Second Breakfast Club' and four heads with pointy ears were just visible over her arms. "They'd have thought, 'Oh, that's horrible,' then gone on with their evening."

"You're Kieran's—"

"Niece," she finished.

He forced a smile. He didn't know why she was making a big deal about it. Any decent person would have done the same. And after seeing the devastation on his fellow Raider's face at the loss of his brother, trying to console the inconsolable, he'd needed something to do. Somewhere to go that wasn't his own empty house. "You know, instead of trying to impale me, you could have answered the door when I rang. And knocked."

"I didn't hear you. I was wearing headphones." She chewed on her plump, bottom lip. "Then I saw the lights again, took them off, and the noises were all around me." She flushed. "I guess it was just you knocking."

"What lights?" His stomach hardened. "What noises?"

She shoved her hands in the back pockets of her jeans, her back arching. He kept his gaze steadfastly on her face. "The lights I can't really describe. Twinkling little sparks, up by the ceiling of the living room? But the noises were probably you on the porch. Although there were some above me, in the attic, I thought."

"I'll check it out." It was probably nothing. Bridget had probably worked herself up into a good scare over a family of squirrels, though he had to admire that her first instinct when frightened wasn't to panic but to pick up a weapon. As strange as that weapon might be. "Where do I access the attic?"

She led him to a trapdoor in the ceiling of the second floor hallway. He pulled it down and an attached ladder extended out. Pulling a slim penlight from his pocket, he started up. "Stay here."

He had to hunch over to clear the area. The low-ceilinged storage space must have driven Kieran nuts with the need to constantly bend over. Odd pieces of furniture had been shoved up here. Some plastic tubs packed full of who knew what. There was an odd stillness to the attic, one that made him grip the flashlight just a little bit tighter. He didn't see any evidence of animals, but it felt like something watched him.

He turned, the thin shaft of laser-like illumination slicing through the darkness. A pale figure flashed in the beam of light, and his pulse leapt.

"See anything?" a voice sounded directly behind him.

"Jesus!" He spun. The light caught Bridget right in the eyes, and she flinched.

"Sorry." He swung the light back to where the form had been, his shoulders slumping. A full length mirror stood wedged into the corner, angled to fit under the sloping roof. He'd been spooked by his own damned reflection. Something else his squad didn't need to know about.

"There's nothing here."

"No raccoons in party hats?" she asked hopefully.

He drew his eyebrows together. "What?"

She sighed. "Nothing. So now I'm hearing things."

"Probably not." He helped her down the ladder and closed up the attic. "Just because no animal has taken up residence in your attic doesn't mean they weren't running around on your roof."

"And the lights?"

"Show me where you saw them." He followed her down to the living room. Ignored the weird-ass game paused on the TV. Of course, she'd like games with trolls and ogres. Dust ran along the edges of the bookshelves. The curtains to the window above the couch were closed, but there was an inch-high gap between the top of the curtains and the top of the window. "Wait here." He went onto the front porch and used his penlight to try to peer through the window. Like before when he'd rung and there'd been no answer, he couldn't see more than just a sliver into the room.

"It's here again," she shouted from the living room.

He returned, sliding his light back into his pocket. "It was just me. I knew you were home, and when you didn't answer, I shone my light through the window. It reflected off the dust motes." He sniffed. "You really should clean in here."

She dropped onto the couch, her whole body sinking into the leather. "Animals and a flashlight. Don't I feel like a moron?"

"You didn't really think you had a ghost, did you?" He sat next to her and patted her leg. "That Kieran was back from the grave?"

She glared at him. "If I'd had a ghost, it wouldn't have been Uncle Kieran. He wouldn't want to scare me."

Which wasn't a denial. He ran a hand through his hair. "Look, I couldn't get a good look at the fire damage, but maybe you shouldn't stay here tonight."

"It's fine." She slumped further down on the couch. "I got lucky. Well, my brother got lucky. It's his house now."

They sat for a moment in silence. "How's your friend?" she asked.

"Driving to his parents right now. Luckily, they don't live far." Losing a loved one was never easy, but to lose someone to murder somehow made it worse. "But his squad is there for him. We all are."

She nodded. "I'm sorry."

They lapsed once more into silence. Tony knew he should get up, go home. But it was comfortable here with his little hobbit. Even with all her rough edges, her sarcasm, for some reason her presence was comforting.

He didn't know how it happened. One moment they were sitting side by side, the next she had one leg thrown over his thighs and was cuddled against his side, his arm around her.

Her hair was as soft as it looked. He pulled the tie from her bun and watched with awe as the apricot tresses fell over her shoulders. He gently ran his thumb under her bruised eye, committing to memory every faint freckle on her face, every tiny wrinkle.

She arched up to him, and it was the most natural thing in the world to scoop his hand under her ass and pull her up and over him. She tasted like dark honey, sweet but with a bite. Her lips were soft under his, opening for him just the way he liked.

He ran his hand up her spine. Back down. It settled on the soft curve of her butt. She was small but perfectly shaped, round just where she ought to be. Thoughts of his friend's heartbreak, of his own squad's problems with the after-action review, drifted from his mind. There was just Bridget.

Bridget. The geeky T-shirt wearing, Pinto-driving, sword-wielding Bridget. His hand froze. So did his tongue.

She leaned back. "What?" she asked, out of breath.

"I'm sorry." He shook his head. "This is wrong."

"Wrong?" Her forehead furrowed. "It feels awfully right to me."

He set her on her own cushion, the sudden space between them chilling his skin. What the hell was he doing? This was Kieran's niece. He wanted to help her, yes, but not fuck her. He shifted his gaze from the plump breasts that heaved beneath her *Lord of the Rings* shirt.

He swallowed. Fucking should definitely be out of the question.

"I don't want to lead you on," he began.

"Donkey balls." She jumped to her feet. "You're such an ass. It's obvious you're attracted to me. It's just as obvious you don't want to be. I'm not your type." She made rabbit-ears around the last word.

She was right. He thought of all the posters he'd had pinned up in his bedroom when he'd been a kid. Alongside the pictures of his sports heroes, there'd been women. They'd all been high-class, business or librarian types. Sexy of course. Usually missing a shirt beneath their suit jackets. Skirts indecently high. But that was his type. Put together. Professional. Always had been.

He knew why. He'd known, even as a young boy, that he'd wanted something better than the trailer park he'd grown up in. Wanted more than the struggling single-mother waitresses that he'd known. Poverty didn't make a woman, or man, any less worthy as a person, but he hated the reminder of his roots. Of weeks of nothing but ramen noodles for dinner. Of the desperation in the eyes around him.

Good or bad, it had formed who he was. What he liked. And he liked women who preferred art shows to online gaming.

He rose. "It's not you."

She rolled her eyes.

"It's not." He gripped the back of his neck. "I just—"

"Save it." She stomped toward the front door. "Since we've established that you think I'm not in your league, I think it best that you stop coming around. I don't need to have my face rubbed in it."

He ground his jaw. There was such a thing as people being too different to be compatible. It wasn't an insult to either of them. But he simply nodded and pulled the door open. "Take care," he said before walking out of her house.

The rectangle of light from the open door was enough to see him to his Cuda. It slowly narrowed until just a sliver of light remained.

He turned. A glimpse of bright hair, the bruised eye, were all that he could see. She shut the door, and then he could see nothing.

It was for the best. He started his engine, the rumble of his V-8 a familiar friend, and focused his eyes on the dirt drive. A longing so intense it stole his breath had him strangling his steering wheel. He was being stupid. Preferences didn't just change overnight. Whatever he was feeling for Bridget wouldn't last.

Driving away now was the best option.

Chapter Eleven

"I'm so sorry." Patty burst through the door of the *Ginger*, shrugging out of her jacket. "My two back tires were flat, and roadside assistance couldn't get to me in less than two hours, and—"

Bridget raised her one free hand. "It's okay. I covered. And I only dropped plates of food on two customers."

A look of horror crossed the waitress's face. "Were they regulars?"

Bridget passed the empty tray over to Patty and untied the half apron from her waist. "I was joking. And it isn't busy yet so if you want to go in back and put your things away, grab a drink, you have time."

And the young woman looked like she could use a drink, and not the soft kind that Bridget was offering. Patty's dark ponytail was off-center with several strands vying to break free. Her jaw was held so tightly it looked like she could grind glass with her teeth. This was the third time Patty had been late in the past two weeks. First her car battery connection had been loose. Then, she'd lost power in her apartment, knocking out her alarm clock. Now tires. The excuses bordered on the unbelievable.

But Kieran had been a good judge of character. If he'd believed Patty and wanted to help her, so would Bridget.

The door swung open again, and a man walked in. He was lean bordering on skeletal, with a shock of dark hair topping a pale face.

A pale, scowling face.

He headed toward Patty. "We weren't done talking."

Casually, so casually Bridget almost didn't notice it, Patty slid behind Bridget, putting her between the two. "I was late for work. I told you that."

Patty held the tray like a shield against her abdomen, and all the hairs on the back of Bridget's neck rose. "Who's this?" She tried to keep her voice pleasant.

"This is Matt Dunkel." Patty paused before adding, "My ex."

Shit. Domestic disputes were never fun to be around. Or safe.

"Thanks again for the ride," Patty said, shifting her weight from foot to foot, "but I have to start work now. I can't talk."

Matt found the nearest empty table and took a seat. "I'll wait. I have to drive you home, after all."

"Uh…" Patty turned wide eyes on Bridget.

Bridget nodded to the back. "Go on, get settled." She caught Karen's eye before turning back to the ex. She was thoroughly tired of ex-boyfriends causing trouble. "Thanks for bringing Patty here, but you don't have to wait around. I'm going to drive her home after her shift."

He narrowed his eyes. His face might have been considered handsome if it wasn't scowling. "She's my girlfriend. I'll drive her."

"She's your ex. She broke up with you." Bridget tapped her fingers against her thigh, trying to keep her cool. If it wasn't men who wanted nothing to do with you, it was men getting way too clingy.

Okay, Bridget had never had the problem of a man getting too clingy with her, but she could imagine it was just as annoying.

"We're working things out." He placed both of his hands flat on the table, his fingers flexing.

Bridget gripped the back of the chair across from him. "No, Matt, there's nothing to work out. She doesn't want you anymore. It's time you moved on."

A look of pure hatred flashed across his face. No one, not even her own ex had ever looked at her with such loathing. "Patty's not your business. She's not going to work here for much longer. She and I were meant to be together."

Warmth from a large body soaked into her back, and the tension in Bridget's shoulders released. The calvary had arrived. Karen must have let Marcus know there might be trouble. Which meant Bridget didn't have to hold back. "Okay, you're out. You are officially banned from *The Limber Ginger*."

Matt's gaze darted from her face to the man standing behind her. "Banned? You have no right. I haven't done anything."

He really hadn't, at least nothing that would sound reasonable for a banning. He hadn't been disruptive nor threatening.

Bridget grinned. But she was the owner now. And with that came privileges. "I don't like your face. That's reason enough for me. Now leave, before we make you."

"And you don't want me to make you," the voice behind her rumbled.

Bridget started. She whipped her head around and gaped. It wasn't Marcus standing behind her. It was Tony.

Matt looked like he wanted to argue, but his gaze caught the row of nine other men who flared out behind Tony the same time Bridget saw them. Individually, each Marine Raider looked like a nice, strong, determined man. As a unit, they looked like monsters, capable of ripping your head off and doing it with a smile.

Without a word, Matt rose to his feet and fled the bar.

Bridget looked at the Raiders. "You've spawned new ones."

Jake's light green eyes crinkled. "This is Delta." He made quick introductions, names Bridget forgot as soon as he said them, then nodded at the door. "Trouble?"

Beside her, Tony sighed. "With Bridget, there always seems to be trouble."

She ignored him. "The ex of one of my waitresses. I'm not sure how much trouble he's going to be yet." She waved Karen over. "Why didn't you get Marcus?"

"Was I supposed to get Marcus?" She nodded hello to the men.

"Yes." Bridget rested her hand on her hip. "I gave you the look. The one that said get some back-up, we might have a problem out here."

Karen pursed her mouth. "We're going to have to work on our looks. I thought yours said talk to Patty about being late again."

Ryan snorted. "Are these tables free? Can I push them together?"

"Go for it." Bridget exhaled. She'd known she'd had back-up when she'd told Matt to take a hike, just not the person or persons she'd been expecting. She darted a glance at Tony. Still built like a Greek god. Still gorgeous.

He folded his long arms. "If you're going to turn that sharp tongue on customers, you really need to get some security."

Still disapproving.

"That sharp tongue is hysterical." Travis dropped into a chair. "'I don't like your face?'" He snorted with laughter. "Ah, Bridget, don't ever change."

"It's not funny." Tony glared at her. "If she says that to the wrong man, there could be a problem."

Bridget gritted her teeth. She was sure Tony's past girl-friends would never insult a man to his face. They'd smile, demur, and delicately extract themselves from any volatile situation.

Bridget wouldn't be friends with the type of woman Tony liked.

"And that's why the *Ginger* caters to you military guys." She turned a bright smile on the squads. "You're always willing to help out in a pinch. Karen, these guys are eating and drinking on the house tonight. As a sincere thank you for assisting this poor, feeble woman who always seems to say the wrong thing." Her smile turned mocking when it landed on Tony.

Ryan whistled. "Maybe Bridget's call sign should be Viper. The way she uses that mouth of hers can sting."

"Why are you called Viper?" Karen asked.

The men chuckled.

"It's a long story." Tony ducked his head as he pulled two chairs out from the table. He looked around for a third, but Karen waved him off.

"I've got to get back to work. The new boss is a slave driver." She winked at Bridget and made her way behind the bar.

"It really isn't that long of a story," Ryan began as Bridget took her seat.

"Yes." Tony glared at him. "It is."

Hmm. Now Bridget really wanted to know. But there was an appropriate time and place. She found the one man at the table who looked like absolute hell. Todd Jakov, she remembered. "I'm so sorry about your brother."

The man nodded, his eyes looking as if they'd been hollowed out by a melon baller. "Thanks."

Bridget didn't know what else to say. The moment of awkwardness was thankfully interrupted by the arrival of some of the girlfriends, Sam and Caroline.

Caroline dumped a large messenger bag on the table and plopped into the chair next to Jake. She blew out a breath, a strand of her pale blond hair rising from her cheek as he leaned over and gave her a kiss.

"Sweetheart." He rubbed the back of her neck. "We can always hire a planner."

"We're spending enough money on the wedding. I don't want to waste more on a planner. Besides"—Caroline smiled as she pointed at Sam—"that's what I have her and Willow for. Free labor."

"And we are on it." Sam kicked her feet up onto Chris's lap with a sigh. "Even if it kills us."

"I didn't know you were engaged," Bridget told Caroline. "Congratulations."

"Thanks." The woman smiled happily. "Oh, you should totally come." She pulled a binder from her bag and flipped to a section tabbed in blue. "Let me just add your name..."

"That's okay." Bridget lifted her hand, as if to ward out the suggestion. She hated weddings. She definitely didn't need to be a pity invite.

Sam yawned. "She'll make you earn your keep, don't worry."

Bridget turned a desperate look on Tony. He'd gotten her into this by pulling out a chair for her. He should get her out.

"It'll be fun." He shrugged. "Jake is the first one of us to get hitched. Can't miss that. And you get a chance to catch the bouquet."

Bridget could feel all the blood drain from her face. Why did he have to bring up the bouquet? She swayed in her seat.

Tony grabbed her shoulder. "Jeez. The idea of marriage is that off-putting to you?"

"Not marriage." Marriage was a fine institution, she was sure. But remembered screams echoed in her head. The sight of rose petals raining down from above. Whoever had invented the tradition of tossing the bouquet was a monster.

A phone beeped. One of the men from Delta squad looked at a message, his expression going flat. He nodded to his men. "We've got to go."

Jake straightened. "You guys are down a man. You shouldn't leave."

Jakov stood. "My leave is over. We're fine."

Jake exchanged a look with the other squad's leader. "This isn't a good idea. It should be us going."

"No, it's good I get out of town before I do something stupid." Jakov downed his drink. "Let's go." Delta squad filed out after him.

Caroline took Jake's hand and murmured something in his ear. He nodded, but his expression didn't change.

The mood at the table had definitely changed. The couples held quiet conversations together. Ryan flirted with one of her waitresses, but it didn't seem like his heart was in it. And she and Tony.... Well, with Chris and Ryan paired up with women of their own, it started to feel like she was Tony's date.

The idea was laughable. Ludicrous even. She should make some snarky comment. Impress upon him that she knew there was nothing between them. But the memory of that kiss lingered in her mind. She pressed her fingers to her lips, her stomach fluttering. Would it be so bad to be on a date with Tony Garcia? Sure, he'd made it clear she wasn't his ideal woman, but she was used to not being a man's ideal. Kevin had made it clear that she fell short in several areas, and they'd still been relatively happy. For a while. Ideals were just fantasies, and she lived in the real world.

She gave Tony a sidelong glance. There was heat between them. When he wasn't annoying the heck out of her, she found him...charming. Maybe he could like her, too?

And maybe she was delusional. He was gorgeous, smart, and protective. He could get his ideal woman. He didn't need to make time with second best. Her heart thudded dully.

Tony rested his hand on the back of her chair. "Listen, I wanted to—"

But whatever he wanted remained unknown. Unprepared to handle whatever he was about to say, Bridget popped to her feet. "Gotta go. Bars don't run themselves." And she fled.

Chapter Twelve

TONY NURSED HIS CUP of coffee, stifling a yawn. Every other man in his squad had the good sense to go home to get some sleep.

Ryan leaned toward the woman seated half on his lap, half on the chair beside him and whispered something in her ear.

Well, almost every other man. But Ryan had never had good sense, at least not when it came to women.

The waitress slapped his shoulder and gave him a wicked smile. "You're bad. And I have to finish closing up." She hopped to her feet. "I won't be long now."

"I'm surprised at you," Tony said when she left.

"Why's that?" Ryan checked his phone before sliding it away.

"Because that's the second time you'll be taking that waitress home. I thought you were a one and done kind of guy."

"I am." He looked offended that Tony had even suggested otherwise. "Marge only looks like that other waitress from last month. The same beautiful dark curls. Now with Judy, the curtains definitely did not match the carpet. She had hard wood flooring if you know what I mean. I wonder—"

"Please just wonder it silently to yourself." Tony rubbed the back of his neck. He still didn't know why he was here instead of at home in bed. The cook, Marcus, was a good guy. He could handle any trouble that came up.

Ryan echoed his thoughts. "Why are you hanging around? Hoping to take little Bridget home? 'Cause I can guarantee that little firecracker came by her hair color naturally. You don't need to check under the hood to confirm. Though it's always more fun checking under the hood." He waggled his eyebrows.

"Jesus, Hawk." Tony gripped his mug, stifling the urge to chuck it at his friend's head. "I don't feel like going home, okay. It has nothing to do with Bridget. I just thought I'd hang out here a while."

"Uh huh."

Bridget came out from the back office and stopped when she caught sight of them. She quirked her head then started their way.

"Just keep your mouth shut," Tony growled at Ryan.

"What are you guys still doing here?" She blew a curl off her cheek. "We closed almost an hour ago."

"Ryan's taking me home," Marge called from a side closet where she was stashing a mop and bucket away.

"I was thirsty." Tony held up his mug. He made a show of taking a big sip, and only felt a little stupid for doing so.

The lights in the back clicked off, leaving them in semi-dark.

"Well, drink up." Bridget held out her hand. "If you're still thirsty, you'll have to take care of that somewhere else."

Tony handed her the mug.

She took it behind the bar and came back with a messenger bag across her shoulder and the waitress with the boyfriend trouble by her side. "Let's go, everyone."

Tony stood and cracked his back. "Where's Marcus? Is he going out the back?"

"He left hours ago." Bridget herded them out the front and locked the door behind her.

Tony pressed his lips together. So much for the women having that guard dog while they closed.

"Thanks again for the ride." Patty pulled the elastic from her hair and rubbed her head. "With the tips I got tonight, I just might be able to afford to have someone come out to reinflate my tires."

"There's not going to be any reinflating of those." Ryan stopped and pointed at Bridget's hideous orange Pinto.

"What the hell?" Bridget rushed over, Tony right behind her. He checked the area around her car while she checked the damage. "They've been slashed," she said. "All four." She let loose with some eye-popping and inventive cursing while Tony pulled out his phone.

After he'd hung up with the police, he turned toward the *Ginger.* "I don't suppose you've put any cameras up?" There was an empty lot on one side of the bar and a strip mall on the other. The shoe store on the corner of the mall didn't have security cameras, either.

Bridget scowled. "You know I haven't."

Tony knelt by the driver's door. "The body's been scratched, too."

"How can you tell?" Ryan asked, earning a glare from Bridget.

His friend wasn't wrong. This car had been born ugly and its wear and tear didn't help the situation. Putting it out of its misery was probably the kindest thing. But rage still churned in Tony's gut. This was Bridget's car. An extension of her. And this had definitely been a message.

Ryan squatted beside him. He squinted. "Someone wrote something here. Love...or...die."

Tony aimed his penlight at where he pointed. "It's 'leave or die,'" he gritted out.

"Are you sure?' Ryan pointed to a scratch. "That looks like an 'o'."

"I know you're supposed to have great eyes, *Hawk*, but that's clearly an e. Asshole just didn't know how to spell." There were a few choice words Tony wanted to make sure the guy knew how to spell. He'd teach him by using his face as a pencil on cement.

"Dude, that's an 'o'." Ryan rubbed his jaw.

"Looks like an 'o' to me, too," Bridget added.

"Besides." Ryan raised one shoulder. "Why would anyone say 'leave or die?' That's too mustache-twirling villain sounding."

Tony gripped the back of his neck. "Why would anyone say 'love or die?'" he barked.

No one could answer that.

"Can you get Patty home while we wait for the police?" he asked.

Ryan nodded. "Patty, why don't you ride with Marge and I'll follow you both. See you tomorrow," he said to Tony.

"I don't know if insurance covers four new tires." Bridget scraped her teeth over her bottom lip.

"I know someone who can give you a great deal." The deal would be damn near free. Tony would make sure of it. "Weren't Patty's tires flat, too?"

"Yes, but not slashed. Someone just let the air out of her back ones. Kids probably." But she didn't sound convinced.

"And if it wasn't kids?"

"Well, her ex seemed awfully Johnny-on-the-spot, and he's definitely having a hard time letting go." She kicked at a piece of gravel. "But exes are always a problem."

He narrowed his eyes, but a cruiser rolled into the lot before he could follow up.

The cops were sympathetic but not hopeful that the tire slasher would be apprehended. Tony managed to convince them that the act might not be random and to take fingerprints from the car, but that was as far as he got. The police agreed to have their tech come to the parking lot first thing in the morning.

When Bridget was in his Cuda, she asked, "You really think I might have been targeted?"

He turned the key in the engine, the angry roar matching his mood. "The fire department only guessed at the cause of your fire, but they don't know a person didn't start it. You've heard noises at your house. Been threatened in the alley behind your business." He headed out of town, his grip tight on his wheel. When he listed it all out, he understood why he'd stuck around tonight. Deep in his gut, he knew Bridget was in trouble. And there was no way in hell he was going to let anything happen to her.

She was Kieran's niece, after all.

"Is there anywhere else you can stay?" he asked.

She crossed her arms. "I'm not uprooting my life for a couple of slashed tires. And even if the fire wasn't an accident, I'm not getting chased out of Uncle Kieran's house."

"Be reasonable. If—"

"I can create boobytraps." She rubbed her chin. "We do it in dungeons all the time. How hard could it be IRL?"

"IRL?"

"In real life."

Jesus. He gripped the steering wheel until his knuckles ached. She was nuts. He turned onto her rutted drive. Absolutely certifiable. She probably thought her sword made a good home defense weapon, too.

He pulled up to the front door.

"Well…" She paused, hand on the door handle. "Thanks for the ride."

"I'm coming in." He climbed out, his gaze scanning the area. "From now on, turn your porch light on when you leave in the afternoon. We can get you a video doorbell, set up cameras around the perimeter."

She trotted after him. "That's all great except for the little matter of paying for it."

"Don't worry about it. I know a guy." He held out his hand. "Keys."

She dug through her bag. "You know a lot of guys."

"It's actually all the same guy." He took the keys and opened the door. "Stay behind me."

She rolled her eyes but for once did as he said. He cleared the downstairs, started for the staircase.

"Wait." Bridget grabbed his arm, her eyes wide. "Did you hear that?"

He listened. Two soft knocks and a scratching sound. "Stay here." He raced for the attic door, jerked the ladder down, and climbed up. He found cover behind an old wardrobe before pulling his penlight out and scanning the area.

His shoulders slowly lowered. Nothing.

"Well?" Bridget's head popped up through the trap door. "Anything?"

"I told you to—" Tony snapped his mouth shut. Arguing with her didn't do any good. "Nothing. Tomorrow you're going to call an exterminator." He followed her down the ladder.

Her gaze tracked him as he climbed down, lingering at a point near his lower back before snapping up to his face. "Oh I am, am I?" She tilted her chin in a way that made him want to shake some sense into her. Or kiss her.

"Do you want to keep hearing sounds above you? Or would you rather help find the squirrel family living here a new home?"

She narrowed her eyes, looking like she wanted to argue more, then sighed. "Well, if they're not paying rent, they get evicted." She slid the ladder up and pushed the trap door closed.

It fell back open.

"Look out." Grabbing her around the waist, he spun her away from the falling ladder.

"Eep!" She clung to his shoulders. Her breasts pressed against the side of his chest. She'd even managed to wrap one leg around his thigh. The heat he felt from between her legs had to be in his imagination.

Her palm drifted down to cover his pec. "You have very quick reflexes." Her teeth scraped against her bottom lip.

His cock punched against the zipper of his pants. He ignored it. This was Bridget. Kieran's niece. There could never be anything long-term between them, and he wouldn't be one of those guys who toyed with a woman just to have a fling. Setting her aside, he shoved the ladder and door into place. "House is clear."

She leaned back against the wall, her glorious hair spilling over her shoulders. "You haven't checked the bedroom up here."

He glared at her. "You're right. I haven't." He stomped into the room. Threw open the closet.

"I've always been scared someone would hide under my bed." She leaned against one of the four massive posts of said bed, obviously not scared at all. She ran her fingers along the dark wood, making his mind go to all sorts of dirty places.

He stamped over and dropped to one knee, peering under. "Nothing."

She crawled onto the covers and dropped onto her side, head propped in one hand. "And on top? Anything interesting on top of the bed?"

Every muscle in his body went hard. If she looked south, she'd see just how interesting he found what was he saw on the bed. Had he thought her a nerd? She was a vixen. A tease. A siren luring him into dangerous waters.

He needed to leave.

He crawled onto the bed instead.

He flipped her to her back. Gripping her hands, he pressed them into the mattress beside her head, then covered her body with his own. "You're being a very bad girl." And he was a weak man. He'd been trained in discipline, but at the moment he couldn't find it in himself to dredge up any of his usual control.

A delighted smile lit up her face, one that warmed him straight through. "Yeah?" she said. "What are you going to do about it?"

Chapter Thirteen

BRIDGET FOUND OUT JUST what Tony was going to do about it. He had her down to her underwear in under six seconds flat. Then his mouth covered hers.

There was no warmup. No soft presses that built to something deeper. Tony took from the moment their mouths touched. His kiss was rough, greedy, right from the start. It was like he had a hunger only she could sate.

She didn't have to worry about her next move, or think about what he might like. Tony told her with his actions. The thrust and parry of his tongue made her spine tingle. The nip of his teeth made her moan. When he was finished exploring her mouth, he raised his head, his dark eyes glowing.

"It's your mouth that gets you into trouble." His fingers danced along the side of her ribs. "I think I've found a way to protect you from yourself."

She sighed, her mind a pleasant muddle. She couldn't remember the last time she'd been kissed that thoroughly. Probably never. "Anytime you want to shut me up by putting yourself in my mouth, you can."

Tony arched an eyebrow.

"Your tongue!" Heat swept from her chest to her face. "I meant your tongue."

Tony chuckled, the sound as rich as a dark chocolate cake.

The air stalled in her lungs. His smile was relaxed. Happy. And it stole her breath.

"You really can't help the words that come out of your mouth, can you?" He ran the tip of his finger over the curve of her breast. Its tip hardened to a peak in response. "When it's not driving me nuts, your audacity is kind of cute."

That sounded promising. She reached for the hem of his shirt and slid her hand underneath. Smooth, warm skin met her touch, along with some very defined abdominal muscles. Mouth watering, she rolled to her knees and tugged the fabric up. It caught on his chin, his nose, then was off, leaving a slightly exasperated looking Tony behind.

A shirtless Tony. And that was the important part. "Sorry," she said, unable to feel true repentance as she gazed at the expanse of caramel-colored yumminess laid out before her. My God, but the man was built. Not in that overly-obnoxious way some body-builders had, with veins popping and muscles that defied physics. But Tony was *strong*, his muscles solid, his body efficient. She didn't even want to think about what his body fat percentage was compared to hers.

She ran her fingers over the dark hair that spanned his chest. Even that looked good on him. By the time she was done exploring, any irritation had faded from Tony's face

"My turn." He deftly unclasped her bra, dropping it off the side of the bed. He cupped her thigh, and with one quick flip of his hand, she was on her back, too many parts of her bouncing right along with the mattress.

Tony grinned. "Have I told you before what a truly beautiful woman you are?"

She huffed out a laugh. "It would mean more if you weren't saying it to my boobs."

He stretched out beside her and cupped one breast. His palm was warm, his thumb teasing. He dragged it around and around her nipple until she thought she would burst if he didn't get to the good stuff ASAP.

"Every part of you is lovely." He pressed his hand flat between her breasts. "Especially in here."

Their gazes locked. Time seemed to pause, stretch. Bridget memorized the location of each golden fleck in his dark chocolate eyes. In that moment, she felt closer to Tony than she ever had to anyone in her life.

And then he ruined it all, because of course, it was Tony. His eyebrows drew together. He opened his mouth. Closed it. Then gave her a smile, one that lacked the sincerity of before, but held plenty of wickedness. His palm skimmed down her abdomen and beneath the fabric of her panties. His finger found her opening, and stroked shallowly inside. "And perhaps in here most of all."

He slid down her body, taking her panties off as he went.

The moment of connection might have been lost but her body didn't care. Her legs opened automatically, her physical needs overcoming any emotional ones.

The first swipe of his tongue had her thanking whoever had messed with her car. If she'd been able to drive herself, Tony wouldn't be here, in bed, with her now.

The second swipe had her thanking God Almighty and the universe for forming in just such a manner that allowed pleasure like this to exist.

Tony peeled her open, blew hot air over her sensitive flesh. And that was when she stopped being thankful and started pleading. He teased her. Tormented her. Brought her close only to nibble soft kisses down her thighs and chuckle at her curses. She almost wept with relief when he finally, finally, took her over the edge.

It was a good thing Kieran's house was out in the middle of nowhere. If it had been in the suburbs, half the subdivision would have heard her screams.

A stupid smile was etched into her face, one she couldn't bring herself to try to get rid of. Tony licked, kissed, and nipped his way up her abdomen, pausing to spend some quality time with her breasts.

She combed her fingers through his hair. She wanted more of this. More time when Tony wasn't looking at her like she had *disaster* stamped across her forehead. Where he succumbed to their attraction without trying to analyze the appropriateness of their coupling.

His finger found her clit just as he drew hard on her nipple.

Her back arched off the bed. More time with Tony's incredible skills.

And if she wanted more, she should contribute something. Show him she could carry half the weight, so to speak.

She shimmied down the bed, her body protesting the absence of his mouth, his hand. When she got where she wanted, she settled in, unbuttoning and unzipping his cargo pants. They didn't need to come all the way off. Down his thighs a bit would do.

"What are you doing?" Tony's voice was wary.

She found the spot she was looking for. "You'll like it. I promise."

"But—" He stiffened then jerked backwards. "Woman! Are you out of your mind?"

Every man she'd been with before had liked this. Sure, she'd only slept with two other men in her life, but the odds were still in her favor. "Just trust me. If I can just reach...."

Tony grabbed her wrists and hauled her hands above her head, dragging her a couple feet up the bed in the process. "Can't you just for once—"

"Lie here passively?" She narrowed her eyes. "Be a *normal* woman? A prim and proper one that you pretend to like?"

"No." He grimaced. "And I don't pretend to like the women I date." At her glare, he hastily added, "I like all types of women. Just, don't do that thing again."

Hmpf. Last week when they'd kissed he hadn't been saying that he liked *all* women. But now that he was in bed with her, he was changing his story. He didn't want the fun times to come to an unceremonious halt.

Which, now that she thought about it, she didn't either. "Maybe it's better if we don't talk."

"Agreed." And so he showed her all the other things he could do with his mouth. The kissing. The sucking. The biting. But the best was his smile when she flipped him to his back and climbed over him.

Okay, he must have let her flip him to his back, but that made it all the sweeter. She scraped her teeth down his neck. Paid extra attention to every nick, scrape, and scar on his body. Finally managed to get his pants completely off.

She must have stilled. Probably had some dopey expression on her face, because Tony cocked both arms behind his head and said, "Like what you see?"

She scowled. "We said no talking." But she did like what she saw. Very much. She took the condom he drew from his wallet and slid it on. Tony was long and hard and she didn't waste one more minute in straddling his lean hips and guiding him inside. When her butt finally reached his thighs, they both sighed.

The connection was amazing. It felt beyond good.

It felt right.

He used his hands on her hips to guide her movements. She reveled in every ridge, every inch as it dragged along her inner walls. Even liked the small pinch of pain when she bottomed out. She dug her nails into his abdomen, needing to brand him. She wanted Tony to remember her long after he went home. See her marks when he tried to convince himself that she wasn't his type of woman.

Tony skimmed a hand up her ribs, pinched her nipple. Electricity arced through her body. Her movements grew jerky. Frantic. Her core tightened, making Tony groan. It was there, but just out of reach. She needed—

Tony splayed one large hand across her butt then rolled, taking her beneath him. He hiked her knee over his shoulder and took over. He threaded one hand in her hair as he drove into her, his eyes hard with determination. "I'm close. Get there."

That was one order she desperately wanted to follow. She slid her hand down between them, found her aching nub, and gave it a lazy circle. Two. Her body tensed. Her neck arched. The orgasm barreled through her like a freight train. She saw nothing. Heard nothing. Only felt, as wave after wave of ecstasy crashed over her.

She was just starting to come down from her high when Tony dug his fingers into her scalp, threw his head back, and roared his release. He ground his groin into hers, setting off small aftershocks in her body as heat flooded her core.

The tension in his body sapped away, and he dropped onto his elbows, his weight pressing her into the mattress without crushing.

She traced a path up his sweat-slicked spine. She wanted to remember this moment, with Tony still semi-hard inside her, his chest hair tickling her breasts with each of his breaths, his scent filling her nose.

Because she knew it wouldn't last. Already she could feel him pulling away. Realizing that he'd made a mistake.

He rolled to one side and scrubbed a hand over his face. "Bridget...."

Whatever he wanted to say next, she didn't need to hear. "Can we just continue this no-talking rule for a couple more minutes?" She swallowed, the back of her throat aching. "Please."

Slowly, he nodded. "I can do that." He wrapped one arm around her and pulled her into his body.

She curled into him, tried to live only in the moment, appreciating the heat he emanated, the slight ruffle of her hair when he exhaled.

As the silence thickened, she realized living in the moment was easier said than done.

Chapter Fourteen

In all his years, Tony never imagined that he'd be working on a Ford Pinto.

"I don't care how much paint you slap on that POS. It's still going to be a POS." Travis sat on the workbench in Tony's converted garage. Tony had bought his house mainly because the old barn had afforded him lots of space to tinker on his cars. But with his four friends crowding about, drinking all his bottled water, and for some reason Ryan doing burpees by the Cuda, it was starting to feel as small as a tuna can.

Chris rubbed his jaw. "I don't know. If I squint and tilt my head, it could almost be considered a classic."

Tony put the final touches on the topcoat and examined his work. The key marks were gone, as were the large patches of rust. It was looking pretty damn close to rolling-out-of-the-factory-fresh, but he didn't know if he could say it looked better. "A Pinto can never be considered a classic. Even if it wasn't built like shit, it doesn't have the lines."

Unlike its owner. Under her weird T-shirts and baggy jeans, Bridget had a body to bring a man to his knees. And it had. Several times in Tony's case.

"There were no prints found on the car?" Jake tossed him a rag.

"Just one set, the same inside and out." Tony wiped his hands. "Bridget's."

Ryan popped up from his last burpee and rested against the Cuda's front end, his chest heaving. "I can't believe you're with a woman with a Pinto. This poor guy"—he tapped the shaker on the Cuda's hood—"will hang his head in embarrassment when he has to park next to that orange monstrosity."

Tony's chest burned. There were more things wrong in that one statement than there were with the original Pinto design. "First of all, my car isn't a guy. She's a lady. And stop dripping your sweat all over Sheila. She doesn't like it."

Travis snorted, but Tony ignored him. "And secondly," Tony said, cracking his neck, "I'm not 'with' Bridget. We're...casual."

His face heated. He was scum. The scummiest of scum. He liked Bridget, they had explosive levels of chemistry, but he still couldn't get his head around the idea of making her his girlfriend. Was she the type of woman he'd want to be the mother of his children? Could he imagine growing old with someone who kept a broadsword in her closet?

Could he take her home to meet Eloise?

His second mom had given so much of her time to him, helping him with homework after she got off work, teaching him to cook, how to change the oil in a car. She was instrumental in him becoming the man he was. The money he sent her senior living home each month could never pay back everything he owed the woman.

Even though she'd had no custodial rights, Elle had set expectations for his teenaged self on the type of person he should associate with. The disappointment in her eyes when she'd caught him cutting school with the local stoner was something he didn't want to see again. Troy might have been a very nice boy, she'd informed him, but Tony had to be careful not to let his dreams become diluted by people who didn't have similar ambitions.

What would Elle think if he brought Bridget around, a woman so unlike everything she had ever wanted for him?

A sour taste filled his mouth. He knew he was an asshole. Knew that Bridget deserved better. What he didn't know was how to stop feeling the way he did.

"Yo, Jake." Ryan bobbed his head at their squad leader. "What would Caroline do if you looked at one of your female friends the way Tony here looks at the barkeep?"

"Cut off my balls and feed them to me," Jake said easily.

"Same here with Sam," Chris added. "And she'd do it with a smile."

"And Willow." Travis grinned. "Though she'd probably pickle them before feeding them to me."

"Oh, speaking of, can you set me up with some more of that plum-licorice jam?" Chris patted his stomach. "I just finished my last jar and I need me some more."

"If we're putting in orders, can I get a couple jars of her cocoa-apricot preserves?" Jake asked. "Caroline loves it."

Tony stared at the ceiling of his barn. "Fuck my life. Can we stop talking about jam please? I need some help."

"With your woman?" Travis asked, his expression working hard but failing to appear innocent.

"She's not my—" Tony bit his tongue. Took several deep breaths. "Look, she's been having some odd things happening around her. Her car being vandalized was the most overt, and it was probably kids, but I want to make sure it isn't anything else."

He had to hand it to his friends. They knew when to stop being assholes.

Travis pushed off of the workbench. "What do you need?"

"Ryan, can you use your computer magic to check out that waitress, Patty's, ex-boyfriend?" He pulled a torn bit of paper from his pocket and handed it to his friend. "I asked Bridget to get his full name."

Ryan nodded.

"Why would someone else's ex mess with Bridget?" Chris's forehead wrinkled.

"I don't know." Tony ran his hand up the back of his head. "But he wasn't friendly to her at the *Ginger*, and the girlfriend had two soft tires that same day."

"Anyone else have a beef with her?" Jake asked.

"She has her own ex who she doesn't like to talk about." Tony frowned. In fact, she was pretty talented at redirecting the conversation whenever he brought it up. "But he's on the other side of the country."

"Like you said, it was probably kids." Chris chewed on his bottom lip.

"Yeah." The guys looked at each other uneasily. There had been a lot of 'it's probably nothing' when each of their girlfriends had been in trouble, too.

Ryan knocked Jake's shoulder. "On a happier topic, what's going on with our status? When are they going to clear us to go active?"

Jake snorted. "Price says it's coming, but we might have to go through some bullshit retraining on the use of deadly force."

"They trained us to kill, and now they're bitching about it." Chris planted his legs wide and crossed his arms. "I never thought there'd be so much bullshit in the military."

"No institution in the world is immune to bullshit." Jake shrugged. "Have to get used to it."

"At least we'll be back to work," Travis said.

Tony's gut clenched. He wanted to go back to work. He believed in their mission and wouldn't want to be anywhere else but besides these men's sides. He only hoped he'd found the punk-ass responsible for harassing Bridget before he did.

And speaking of.... "I'm going to get Bridget's car back to her." He pulled out his phone and dialed her number. It went straight to voicemail. "Whenever I find out where she is."

"It's sad that I know where your girl is and you don't." Chris stretched. "It really shows a lack of awareness on your part."

"Shows a lack of something at least," Ryan muttered.

Tony planted his hands on his hips. "Are you going to tell me or do I have to guess?"

"I'll do better. I'll show you." Chris dug his keys from his pocket and headed for the barn door. "Follow me."

He paused and turned back around. His nose wrinkled. "But don't follow too close. I don't want anyone to think I have a friend who drives a Pinto."

Tony balled up his towel and chucked it in his direction, but Chris was already gone. All that remained was his laughter.

Chapter Fifteen

When no one was hitting back at her, punching was actually kind of fun. Bridget struck the heavy bag where she thought someone's kidney might be. Someone Tony's height, at least.

"It's a great way to work out frustrations, isn't it?" Sam grinned over from her own bag. Sweat trickled down her friend's red face, and Bridget assumed she looked about as rough.

"Yep." She experimented with a right hook. Almost as therapeutic as swearing. And she'd had lots to swear about these past days. From the first time they'd slept together, Tony had taken her plea not to talk as an eternal vow. They were in a holding pattern, neither of them wanting to broach the topic that hung over their heads like Damocles sword. Because as soon as one of them brought up the issue of their incompatibility, fun time was over.

Sam threw some wicked looking knees into the bag, making the chains holding it rattle.

"Whoa, you okay over there?" Bridget asked.

Sam used her boxing glove to try to push loose hair off her cheek. She wasn't very successful. "Yes." She blew at the hair from the corner of her mouth until it fluttered off her face. "I'm just worried for Chris and the other guys. This after-action review is taking longer than they expected. Not that I want him to go back in the field necessarily, but it's his job and he loves it."

"Yeah." Bridget elbowed the bag. "I can tell Tony's not happy about it, either. Although he has made a very handy chauffeur these past couple of days that he's had my car."

"Tony has your car?"

"Putting on new tires and fixing some of the damage to the body." Her heart warmed. She'd never felt so taken care of, and she and Tony weren't even a couple. She couldn't imagine how well he'd treat a woman he was serious about.

Sam executed a jab/cross combination. "Why is it always the cars they go after?" she muttered.

Bridget eyed her curiously, but before she could ask what she meant, Sam said, "Anymore ghost sightings? I think you should get one of those EVP...EMP...whatever, one of those ghost detector devices. I don't think they're very expensive."

Bridget pursed her lips. She could just imagine Tony's reaction if he found her trying to scan the electromagnetic fields in the house. She should add a ghost detector to her shopping list. Seeing his expression would be funny as hell. "No more weird occurrences. If there is a ghost, Tony is keeping it away." Although there was that one spot by the couch that always seemed cooler than the rest of the room. She probably needed to reseal the window.

Sam stopped abusing the boxing bag. "Tony is over that much, huh?"

Bridget's cheeks heated. "We're just having fun. It's nothing serious."

"Riiiight."

"Sticks!" John called out. "One per person."

Bridget stripped off her boxing gloves. "It's not. I'm not his type, and he's not mine."

Sam laughed. "Hot. Kind. Smart. Adventurous. What exactly is he missing?" She tossed her gloves in the direction of her tote bag.

"Imagination." Although he had been pretty imaginative when it came to their naughty times. But still. "I don't think he's ever read a fantasy novel, and I live on them."

Sam shrugged. "A man is allowed a flaw. If they were perfect, it would make us too insecure to be happy with them."

Bridget pondered that as she trotted over to the carrel that held the escrima sticks and chose the fattest one she could find. She didn't want the fun times with Tony to end. When he held her, it was like nothing in the world could get to her, she was that happy. Could they have a future?

She swished the stick in a quick figure eight, making Sam dodge out of the way. Damn Tony for being the one guy who made her feel that way.

"Box pattern." The instructor moved around the room, observing their technique.

"Let's go slow, okay." Sam held her stick up warily. "You tend to—"

"Hiya!" Bridget swung at Sam, making sure her friend had time to block, but enjoying that small shriek of fear just the same. Escrima was the one thing that came easily to her in class. Sam could beat her up with every other technique, but put a sword-like object in Bridget's hand and she finally dominated.

"Yeah, yeah yeah!" John stood beside them, nodding approvingly. "Keep the pattern going. Faster."

Bridget grinned as she went through the striking and blocking motions. It was so rare that she got praise for anything physical. Well, Tony *had* said some nice things, but that was only when they were in bed. She gritted her teeth. And thinking about Tony only pissed her off again.

"Aim for the temple," John told Sam.

Sam grimaced. "I don't want to accidentally hurt her."

"You won't. You're not going one hundred percent, and she's good at blocking." He nodded approvingly. "In real life, if someone's attacking you, you can't be afraid to go for the vital spots. It's not your fault they're dead."

"Words to live by."

Bridget and Sam both started at the voice, and their sticks paused in mid-air. Chris strode up, Tony right behind him, and shook the instructor's hand. "Good to see you. Been awhile."

"Yeah." John nodded to Tony. "When are you going to get your ass back in jiu-jitsu class?"

"Trying to make time." Chris leaned down and kissed Sam's cheek. "Do you mind if we join in for the last few minutes?"

"Sure." The instructor slapped Tony's shoulder. "It will be nice to give these women targets they can really beat up on. Sticks away!" he called to the class. "RTS, one through five."

Bridget looked at her stick. She looked at Tony. He was wearing chinos, a blue T-shirt, and white socks, and he looked good enough to eat. Even without shoes, he looked like he'd stepped out of a magazine. She wanted to muss him up. Make him look as tired and dirty as she knew she did. Or at least give him one good whack.

She put her stick away instead. "Why are you here?" she asked after rejoining him on the mat.

"I have your car." He watched the pair next to them work the move, nodded, and threw her a slow straight punch. "The cops didn't find the prints of the person who vandalized it unfortunately."

She stepped to the side and performed the punch/kick combination, giving Tony light taps. "Is Gimli okay?"

Tony rolled his eyes, but a smile tugged at the corners of his lips. "Your car is as okay as a Pinto can be." He feinted left. "I want to talk to you about your ex."

Bridget stumbled. "What? Why?" That was a conversation she didn't want to have with anyone, especially Tony. Kevin was proof that she was a disaster. Tony didn't need to see any more evidence of it.

"Could he be behind your car? The fire?"

"No. He's in California." Block, kick, punch. She focused on the movements.

"There are planes." He easily blocked her. "How badly did it end between you two?"

"Look." She paused, chest heaving. "Trust me. It wasn't Kevin." His weapons were words and lawyers. It would never even cross his mind to slash her tires or key her car.

Tony pursed his lips. "You also thought you had a ghost. You don't necessarily have the best judgment."

Her next kick was a bit lower from the belt than she was supposed to be aiming at. Harder too.

Tony grabbed her foot before it made contact, and before she knew what was happening, she was flat on her back with Tony rolling on top of her.

"That wasn't very nice," he said mildly.

Perhaps not. But then, either had he been. She shoved his shoulders but it was like trying to push a boulder uphill. "Don't make fun of my ghost."

He pushed a strand of hair off her cheek. "You didn't really think your house was haunted, did you?"

Because, of course, none of Tony's perfect women would be absurd enough to believe in things that go bump in the night. She tried to get him off of her with the hip bump they'd learned.

The movement only managed to put a wicked gleam in his eyes and bring heat to her own core. Every part of him was just so solid, and big, and....

He lowered his head, his breath dancing across her mouth.

Someone cleared his throat loudly next to them. "Class is ending," Chris said, laughter in his voice.

Sam leaned into his side. "I don't think we learned that move here, Bridget."

Face heating, Bridget pushed at Tony's shoulders again.

This time, he allowed himself to be moved, but he took his time about it. He rolled to his feet then reached down to pull her to hers. "I'm not sure how effective any of these moves would be on a man my size if Bridget tried to work them."

Quick as a snake, well as quick as one who might have just eaten a big meal and was caught napping in the sun, she jumped onto Tony's back and wrapped her arm loosely around his throat. "In my training as rogue in my role playing games, I've learned to use deception to vanquish my foes. Lure them in with a kiss then go for the jugular."

"Oh my God," Tony said as Chris and Sam laughed. "You're hopeless." He shook his head as he plucked her off his back and set her on her feet. "Hopeless and adorable."

Her heart danced an Irish jig. That look in his eyes, it wasn't the usual one where she could see him comparing her to his ideal and measuring every place where she fell short. This one held warmth. Fondness even.

Maybe time was all he needed to realize he didn't actually want his ideal. Maybe it was best not to have 'the talk' and push him to make a decision. Maybe she could slowly and stealthily win him over.

And maybe she was just a little bit pathetic. Where was her pride? Her self-respect? She shouldn't have to seduce a man to like her against his better judgment.

"Can I take you to an early dinner?" Tony asked. He led her to where their shoes were stacked, his hand warm on her lower back. "I know you've wanted to try that new Cajun place."

And just like that, all her pride and self-respect flew out the window. So she wasn't Tony's ideal woman. He didn't know a troll from an orc, which wasn't ideal for her, either. But he was more thoughtful than Kevin had ever been, and she didn't want to let this go. Not yet.

Tony could find his perfect mate later. Right now, he was with her. And she wanted to spend as much time as she could with him before he moved on.

Chapter Sixteen

THE HAMMER PUNCHED A hole through the drywall, flakes of white debris flying through the air. Tony pursed his lips and slid a glance to his right. Chris was still hunched over a pallet in the corner of the room. Maybe he hadn't noticed. Maybe Tony could patch it before—

"Nice aim, asshole." Chris laid another plank of pine flooring. "Next time, aim for the wall and maybe you'll hit the nail by mistake."

Tony dropped his head forward. Exhaustion burned at his eyes, so he closed them, too. He didn't need to be here. Yes, he'd promised Chris he'd help him remodel this cottage in his spare time, but Chris was a jackass, and promises to jackasses didn't really count.

"His aim is fine when his eyes are open."

Tony started. When had Jake arrived?

Their squad leader looked up from his phone. "Next time don't swing when you're mid-yawn."

Tony would have agreed but he wouldn't get anything done if he waited until he wasn't yawning. Between staying up late to make sure Bridget got home okay from closing the bar and waking up early for PT with the squad, he was wiped.

Jake ran his hand along the newly-installed wainscotting on the far wall. "This is really coming along. When are you going to put it on the market?"

"I'm not." Chris stood and stretched his back. "Maddie is applying for emancipation so she'll legally be an adult. She's been saying she wants to get her own place and I'm going to give this to her." He shrugged. "Of course, she's welcome to stay with Sam and me when Sam moves in, but I don't think she'll want to."

Tony frowned at the hole in the wall he'd made. If he'd known this place was for Sam's little sister, he would have taken more care. The girl was practically a little sister to all of them.

"Sam's moving in with you?" Jake asked.

"Yep, I finally convinced her." Chris smiled. "And this place is only two blocks from my house so the sisters will be close."

"Congratulations." Jake's phone beeped, and a pained look crossed his face when he looked at the screen. "When you and Sam decide to make it official, take her to Vegas. This wedding is killing me."

"Is Caroline changing her mind about the color scheme again?" Tony bit back his grin. He knew his friend wanted to make his fiancée happy. He also knew Jake could give a fuck less about what color flowers were on the tables and if they should match the tablecloths.

"She wants..." Jake swallowed. "She wants us to learn a special dance to...perform for our guests." He looked like he wanted to vomit just saying the words.

Wisely, Chris and Tony didn't comment or laugh.

Chris walked over to a cooler and pulled out a bottle of water. "Well, your advice should go to Travis. I caught him looking at rings, and he says he's going to propose to Willow after you get married."

"Why is he waiting?" Jake asked.

"Doesn't want to steal attention away from your wedding." Chris straddled a sawhorse and sat down.

Jake's eyebrows drew together. "I don't give a fuck when he proposes."

Chris shrugged. "He said his sister told him Caroline might be upset." He held up his hand. "From my understanding, it's a girl thing."

Tony leaned against the wall. Another squad member getting married, and Travis would be a dad now, too, with Willow's little girl coming along as part of the package. It was hard to imagine. Just last year they were all single and now three of his friends were settling down. Ryan was a lost cause and would remain a bachelor forever, but Tony had hope for himself.

His phone rang, and he couldn't help the smile when he saw Bridget's name. He strode from the room as he answered.

"Thanks for the bumper sticker," she said. "I love it."

When Tony had seen the sticker of the nine figures hiking, one with a distinctive pointed hat and staff, along with four hobbits and a dwarf, he knew he had to get it for her. "I figured Gimli would like to have his friends around. Also, covering your car in stickers can only improve its appearance." He would never dream of putting a sticker on Sheila, but that was different. She was a classic.

"I choose not to be offended by that."

Tony chuckled. This was new for him. He'd never had a relationship where he just enjoyed the moment with a woman. They both knew he wasn't looking for long-term with Bridget, and they both were happy to just have fun in the here and now.

A soft ping came over the line. "Hold on a sec," Bridget said. "Huh. That's weird."

"What? And are you driving? Don't be looking at your texts and driving."

A heavy breath gusted over the line. "I'm stopped at the red light at Washington. You know it takes forever. It's fine. But...."

"But what?"

"This is just weird. My phone is notifying me that an air tag is detected near me. I don't know what to do with that information."

"An air tag? Like what people put on their phones or luggage in order to find them if they're lost?" Tony frowned. "Drive another couple of blocks. It's probably just picking up a phone in a car next to you."

"Okay. The light's changing." There was a pause. "So how's the house coming? It's hard to imagine that Chris has spare time to flip houses on his off hours. How long has he been doing this?"

"Several years now," Tony said, impatient. "Well? Did the notification go away?"

"No, still there."

Chris and Jake strolled in from the next room, going silent when they saw him. Chris mouthed 'What's up?'

Tony quickly told them about the air tag.

Chris's face hardened. "I've heard some people are placing those devices on cars in order to track them. After what happened with Sam and Maddie, I've learned all the ways creeps work when stalking people."

Dread swirling in his gut, Tony headed for the kitchen where he'd left his keys, all traces of fatigue wiped from his body. "Do you know where the police station is downtown? Go there. Wait for me in the parking lot."

"Tony, I'm sure it's nothing. Don't you think—"

He cut her off. "Just like your tires were nothing? Everything will be fine"—he'd make damn sure of it—"but do this for me. Go to the police station. I'll meet you there."

She sighed. "Fine, but you're going to have to explain this one to the cops. After all the interactions I've had with them lately, they're going to think I'm some attention-nut doing these things to myself."

"Don't worry about the cops." Because if Tony was right, if someone had put a target on Bridget's back, he wouldn't be looking to the police for help. They'd only get in his way.

No, if someone was after Bridget, Tony would take care of the asshole himself.

Chapter Seventeen

"YOU'RE A PALADIN. YOU'RE alignment is lawful good."
Bridget shoved a strand of hair off her face and glared at
Chris. "You can't just kill him."

"He lied to us." Chris pointed at the quivering female
character on the TV. "When his wife sees we're serious,
maybe she'll tell us what we need to know."

"His logic is sound," their thief said over their headsets.
"Don't you want the intel?"

Desperately, just not the intel her friend was talking
about.

It had taken Tony over two hours to find the air tag
placed on Gimli. The police were taking it seriously, asking
the fire investigator to look into the cause of her fire again,
saying they'd increase patrols around the *Ginger* and her
home.

It was unnecessary. Once Tony had found the tag, she'd been under virtual lockdown. If he wasn't with her, one of his squad members was. She liked the guys, she did, but if she didn't have some alone time pretty damn soon she was going to go after them with her sword. She needed to find out who was harassing her.

She launched a minor attack on the innkeeper's wife, and blood spurted from her wound.

Chris arched an eyebrow.

"Pain will give her another incentive to talk." She rolled her eyes at the squawking over the headsets. "If no one else is going to follow the rules, I'm not going to, either."

Chris clapped her on the shoulder. "'Atta girl. Now look out for that troll. Kill him. Kill him!"

"What the hell is going on?" The voice was muffled by her headset, but the disdain in it was clear.

"Hold up," she told her gaming group before taking off her headset and turning to Tony. "Hi. I didn't hear you come back."

"I did." Chris pointed to his left ear which remained uncovered by the headset. "One thing your car is not is stealth. That engine could wake the dead."

"It's not my approach you need to worry about." Tony looked at the TV screen which Bridget had hooked up to her computer and frowned. "And listening with one ear doesn't instill confidence in me that you're taking the job of watching Bridget seriously."

"I'm a job now?"

The men ignored her. "I know you're in a pissy mood," Chris said, his expression going flat, "but don't take it out on me. If I say I'll take care of your girl, I'll take care of your girl."

Was she his girl? It felt like it, and she liked the feeling. But they still hadn't really talked.

The tension in the room grew until Tony hissed out a breath, his shoulders inching down from his ears. "You're right. I'm sorry. You're not the one I'm angry with." He turned his stare on her.

Bridget looked behind her but there was only wall. "What? Why are you mad at me?"

"I talked to Karen when I finished installing the security system at the bar." He crossed his arms over his chest. "She says you're going in to work tonight."

"Well, yeah. It's Karen's night off."

There was some muffled noise from the headsets, and Chris murmured into his mic, "There's some dispute about whether *Deathmantle* is going in to work tonight."

"There's no dispute. I'm going." She split her glare between Chris and Tony. "I can't hide out in this house forever. I need to make money to eat." And speaking of, the chip bowl was empty. She pushed to her feet and stalked to the kitchen.

"It won't be forever." Tony stood in the doorway, leaning against the jamb with one shoulder. "And I already cleared it with Karen. She says you'll owe her a nice vacation after this, but she'll work every night until this is resolved."

Heat rose from her chest to fill her face. "*You* cleared it with Karen?"

"Yes." A pleased smile rose to his lips. The man was completely unaware of the danger he was in. "You have nothing to worry about now. I've got it covered."

"*You* have it covered." She stomped past him, ignoring how adorable he looked when he got confused.

"Now she's repeating everything he's saying back to him," Chris murmured into his headset. He chuckled. "You're right, *Elf Lord*, that's never a good sign."

Bridget glared at Chris as she tore open her bag of chips and dumped them into the bowl. Her wrath could encompass many.

"Wait, are you mad I talked with Karen?" Tony asked from close behind her.

"Realization is dawning," Chris continued his play-by-play to the gaming group. His brows drew together. "No, I won't tell you what she's wearing. Your friends are pervs," he said to her.

She spun back to Tony. "Look, I appreciate that you're trying to help me. I do. But you can't manage my employees. That's my job. And you can't tell me where I can and can't go. That's my job, too."

His dark eyes flashed. "I didn't think I'd need to tell you. I'd have thought it would be obvious that you'd need to stay home until we catch this guy."

"So, what?" She swept her hand to the TV. "You expect me to do online role playing all day?" Her anger helped her ignore the fact that playing all day actually sounded kind of nice. For a while.

His lip curled. "Well, you could find a better hobby."

Blood pounded in her ears. Chris's voice sounded only faintly as he relayed this latest to the gaming group. "Now don't get your panties in a twist, *Glorfindel*. Viper might be an asshat, but he's like a brother to me. I will have to defend his honor if you finish that sentence." He paused. "Oh, it's a great story how he got his call sign. He—"

"A better hobby?" Bridget interrupted.

"She's repeating his words again," Chris murmured into his headset. He straightened. "I don't even know what part of the anatomy that is but that sounds filthy. I told you not to insult my boy. You're gonna have to die now." He started clicking away furiously on his controller.

"I didn't mean better," Tony started, but Bridget wasn't having it. She turned on her heel and flounced from the room. She didn't know where she was going, but the staircase was there so she climbed it to the second floor.

Footsteps pounded after her. "I didn't mean better. I just meant you could take the opportunity to branch out a little. Discover other hobbies you might be interested in."

She tried to slam the bedroom door behind her, but Tony was there, catching it with his palm before it could smack into his face. He slid inside and closed the door behind him. "Bridget." His voice was soothing, calm, like someone trying to tame a wild animal.

It only incensed her more. She dug her nails into her palms and tried her best to keep her own voice level. "I will never be the white wine drinking, heels and pearls wearing kind of woman you want."

"I don't want you to be anyone other than yourself."

He sounded so sincere she almost believed him. But their past history told her differently. She paced in a semi-circle around the bed. "When you eventually settle down, who do you picture by your side? Someone like your last girlfriend, or someone like me?"

He ran a hand through his chocolate hair and started some pacing of his own. "I'm not thinking about settling down."

A cop-out if she ever heard one. "I know why you get annoyed when you see me playing my games. When I wouldn't throw out my favorite T-shirt."

"It had a hole in it," he objected.

"They're all reminders that I'm not the classy woman you tell yourself you want. But this is who I am." She pointed at the dragon on her current t-shirt. "And this is who you take to bed each night, desperate to get inside me. So what does that say about you?"

"With all the grief you give me, it says head trauma."

Bridget rolled her eyes.

He stepped into her path and gripped her shoulders. "Yes, I want you. And yes, damn it, I like you. A lot."

"But you wish I were different."

He gave her a little shake. "I didn't say that. I can't even imagine you different. You're absolutely unique. I like you. I want to be with you right now. Why isn't that enough?"

An invisible vise closed around her chest. Why wasn't that enough? Why was she pushing this?

Her heart knew. Because she was past the point of 'like.' She was falling ass over teakettle for this man. And he just saw her as temporary.

His eyes darkened. He dragged her close so each heave of her chest brushed against his. "I'll make it be enough." And before she could wonder what that meant, he slammed his mouth on hers.

Chapter Eighteen

THE KISS WAS MESSY. Uncivilized. Teeth knocked. Lips gnashed together. Tongues clashed. But it was real. Probably the most honest kiss Tony had ever given her. The need she felt from him was unmistakable. The want. The frustration.

Tears built behind her eyelids even as her body melted against his. Tony might not realize it, but she knew. This was good-bye. And it broke her heart.

He broke away just long enough to rip her T-shirt over her head. Her hair was knocked loose from its clip and swung against her bare shoulders. A shiver raced down her spine as Tony swung her into his arms and carried her to the bed.

She memorized the lines of his face as he took off the rest of her clothes and worked on his own. The long, straight nose. His beautiful dark eyes. The stubborn set of his jaw.

So stubborn, she thought, as he took her lips once again. He seemed determined to prove to her what he felt. Now only if he could prove that to himself.

His hands glided over her every curve. His fingers tangled in her hair. And when he pushed inside her, she knew she'd never feel anything so wonderful in her life again. She wrapped her arms around him, tucked her face into his throat, and closed her eyes so no tears could escape.

Each thrust stretched her. Molded her so they fit perfectly. Made her his. But she was a possession he didn't truly want. Her chest felt like it would split open even as tingles gathered low in her belly. But that pain soon ebbed. It couldn't withstand the pleasure that gathered in her body. The reprieve was temporary, she knew it, but she welcomed the mindless oblivion that came when he pulled her head back and pressed his teeth into the base of her throat. She'd feel that mark long after he had moved on. Bliss coursed through her, rolling through her extremities to curl her fingers and her toes.

She gasped for breath, knowing that as soon as her body cooled, her heart would burn with loss once more.

Tony framed her face with his palms. He held himself deep inside her, still hard. "Again." He started moving.

A sad smile curved her lips. It was a temporary reprieve. But she'd take it.

Tony wasn't willing to have it end. He didn't quite understand the look in his Bridget's eyes, but he didn't like it, and he was doing his damned best to fuck it away.

He rocked into her gently. He was too damn close, and he needed to think about something, anything, other than Bridget's tight, wet sheath. The way her bright hair looked splayed across the pillow. The arch of her neck when she came.

Fuck, that didn't help. He tried to focus on that stupid game she played online with her friends. the ridiculous warrior character she made as her avatar. It didn't work. Bridget was adorable as hell when she went full nerd.

He brought up the image of her charging at him with a sword. And groaned. That only brought him closer to the edge. She might only stand hobbit-high, but she had the heart of a warrior, and that did all sorts of things to him.

Even the memory of the night she had traded shots with Marcus after the cook's shift was over did nothing to diminish his feelings for the woman. She could drink any other woman and most men he knew under the table, and for some reason, God help him, that did it for him. She didn't get ugly drunk like his mom, but sweetly buzzed. None of his other girlfriends had even gotten tipsy around him. He'd thought he'd admired their restraint, but now he realized he'd never really known their true selves. They'd been so restrained they'd never fully shared themselves with him.

Bridget shared everything. She was completely open about her idiosyncrasies, and, God, but he loved her for them.

His eyes flew open.

He loved her. That was why the sex between them was unlike anything he'd ever felt. Being inside a woman was always amazing, but being inside the woman you loved was another level he hadn't known existed. All the ways she differed from what he thought was what he wanted were all the things he loved about her. He'd just been too trapped in his past to see it.

He rolled his hips, keeping his thrusts shallow and slow. He trailed kisses from her lips down her throat. He licked over the small mark he'd left with his teeth. Life was a kick in the nuts. All your plans, your goals, everything you've worked for, changed in an instant when the right person barreled into your life.

He threaded his fingers with hers and stretched her hands above her head. At the end of each thrust, he ground his pubic bone into her clit. Her eyes flew open, and he savored the pleasure he saw in them.

The skin at the base of his spine prickled a warning. "Give it to me," he growled. He wasn't going without her. He nipped at her jaw, her collarbone. When his teeth found her nipple, she arched into him with a cry. Her core clamped around his cock.

Relief mixed with ecstasy. His balls drew tight, and his tension exploded out of him in waves of pleasure.

He collapsed to his side and held her close, enjoying each dwindling spasm until their bodies settled.

He kissed her forehead.

"Don't." Bridget stiffened and pulled away, leaving him cold.

"Don't what?"

She rolled to the other side of the bed and scooted off. Her shoulders had a set to them he'd never seen before. "Don't pretend. This was just sex. Sweet kisses on my forehead aren't a part of that."

He jackknifed up as she gathered her clothes. "Just sex?" A pit of nausea opened in his stomach. He'd just had the most transcendent experience of his life and she thought it was *just sex*?

"I can't do this anymore." Her words were muffled by the shirt she pulled over her head. Her face popped out over the collar, and its lack of expression scared Tony more than any battle had in his life. "We're not meant to be, and I don't want to prolong a pointless relationship any longer."

"It's not pointless." His voice was so low he barely recognized it. He climbed out of bed and stood in front of her. "I love you, Bridget. I want a future."

She blinked. Then turned her back to slip into her jeans. "Unbelievable. Now that I'm cutting off sex you think you have feelings for me. Don't worry, they'll pass."

He grabbed her shoulders and spun her around. "This has nothing to do with sex and everything to do with you and me. I've been an ass. I know it. But you don't get to tell me if my feelings are real or not."

Her throat rolled. "You might think you love me now, that you can see past all my personality traits that you think are flaws, but it won't last. Pretty soon you'd be looking at me and wondering why I can't act like a proper woman. Wear a dress once in a while. Straighten my hair so it's not such a frizzy mess."

He dug his fingers into her hips and yanked her close. "You look better in t-shirts, and don't you dare touch your hair. I love your messy curls."

The bedroom door rattled in its frame, and Bridget jumped.

"What?" Tony shouted, not taking his eyes off of her.

The door swung open. "Get your pants on," Chris said. "Just got a call from Psych. We're on."

Tony's pulse raced. No. Not now. He couldn't leave Bridget like this. "We're suspended. Delta took our place."

"Not anymore." Chris's nostrils flared. "And Delta needs our help."

Tony had to force his fingers to relax their hold on Bridget. He was probably leaving bruises as it was. He nodded. "Give me a minute."

"Only one," Chris said and closed the door.

"When I get back—"

"When you get back, please don't come to the *Ginger* anymore." She bent and handed him his pants. "I know it's not your kind of place anyway."

He yanked on his clothes. "When I get back, we're finishing this conversation." He'd make her see. He had to.

A horn blared from the front drive.

"Fuck." He had to go. It was his job. But he'd never regretted being at someone else's beck-and-call more than right now. "Stay safe. Don't take chances. We'll talk when I get back."

"It won't make any difference," she said as he strode to the door.

Bridget hadn't known him or the other Raiders long. They were mission-focused. Did whatever was necessary to get the job done. And convincing this woman to take another chance on him had just become his primary goal.

He gave her one last lingering look. "Like hell it won't."

Chapter Nineteen

THE *GINGER* SEEMED OFF tonight. There were the same food and drink orders, the same shrieks of laughter, but it all felt hollow. Forced. Or maybe that was just Bridget.

For three days she'd tossed and turned over her decision to end it with Tony. Three days where she'd wondered what it would be like to never see that smile of his aimed her way again. To never feel his touch. To not have that feeling of security knowing he'd always be there to help, whether she wanted him to be or not.

And speaking of....

She wended her way through the tables until she reached the back corner. The man was still there, a different face than the night before, but made of the same type. Muscles for miles. Stoic expression. Watchful eyes. "Have you heard anything?"

His reddish-blond eyebrows drew together. "Ma'am?"

"About Tony and his team?" None of her worries about the should-she-or-should-she-not of her relationship with Tony had compared to the one of knowing he was overseas putting himself into a deadly situation. All of this secrecy and no phone calls business was bullshit.

Okay, necessary for national security and all that, but still bullshit.

"I don't know what you're talking about," the big man said.

She planted her hands on her hips. "Don't give me that crap."

"Swear jar," Patty said as she bustled past with drinks in her hands.

Bridget frowned. She didn't think crap was strong enough to qualify for the swear jar, but that wasn't important now. "You and your friends have been watching me for several days now. I'm assuming Tony asked you to look after me while he was away. If I'm wrong, let me know and I'll call the police right now since I appear to have attracted new stalkers."

He grimaced. "My name's Henry McAvoy. And I'm just doing Viper a favor."

Her heartbeat drummed in her chest. After basically getting kicked out of her bed, Tony still did his best to watch out for her. "And? Have you heard anything? Is he okay?"

Henry's face blanked. "All I know is he is out of town. That's all I need to know."

She ground her teeth so hard her jaw hurt. "I don't know how any woman can be with any of you guys." The blood pressures of the wives and girlfriends of special forces operatives must be through the roof.

"It is a mystery, ma'am."

Bridget grunted. "Do you want more coffee?" She indicated his empty mug.

"Thank you, ma'am."

She filled him up then made the rounds of the bar, chatting with some regulars. She felt too unsettled to sit behind her desk to work on next month's budget. There was an itch between her shoulder blades that wouldn't go away. She was full of so much nervous energy she had the urge to put on some sweats and go for a run.

She'd never had that urge before.

When she caught sight of Patty's ex slithering in through the front door, she was almost glad. This was a problem she could attack, and do so with pleasure. "You've been banned from the *Ginger*," she said just as he was lowering himself into a chair at a two-top table in the corner.

Patty beelined over to them. "It's okay, Bridget. He called earlier, and I agreed to talk with him on my break."

Matt gave her a smug grin.

Bridget took Patty's arm and drew her aside. "What are you doing?"

Patty pressed her serving tray to her abdomen, her shoulders hunching. "There was a flood at my apartment. I can't afford to move again. Matt's asked me to come back to live with him. I don't have a choice."

"Twat waffle!"

Patty started.

"Not you." Bridget dug some change out and slapped it in Patty's hand. "For the swear jar. Look, have you considered that Matt is the one causing all these problems with your apartments? You can't go back to him."

She swiped the back of her palm across her cheek. "Every place needs first and last month's rent, and I'm losing my security deposit on this place. I can't do it anymore."

Bridget glared at the bastard over Patty's shoulder. "You can stay with me."

"What?" Patty shifted back and forth.

"Stay with me." Bridget nodded. It was the right thing to do. It's what Uncle Kieran would have wanted. "Kieran's house has plenty of room. You can stay as long as you need until you get back on your feet. And you can finally kick your ex to the curb for good."

Patty bounced on her toes. "I'm a good roommate. I cook and I can keep things really clean and—"

Bridget cut her off with a laugh. "You don't have to sell yourself. You already have the room. And since we'll have separate bathrooms, I think we can do this without killing each other." She hoped. And she didn't say it, but having another person in that house with everything that was going on would be a relief. "Now, do you want me to tell Matt where he can stick his offer, or do you want to do it?"

"I'll tell him." She bit her lip. "I don't think he'll make a scene here."

"If you need back-up, just wave." Bridget watched with some amount of anticipation as the waitress approached her ex. The way she was feeling, she wouldn't mind getting into a confrontation with the jerk. And thanks to Tony, she knew she had back-up of her own if things got out of hand.

"Ms. Sullivan?" A man in a dark suit stood next to her.

"Yeah?" She didn't take her eyes off Patty and Matt. She could tell the exact moment Patty had said she wouldn't be moving back in with him. Her ex's face turned all kinds of ugly when things didn't go his way.

"I'm Special Agent Grimes with the FBI." The gold badge he held out finally drew her attention. "I'd like to speak with you about your employment at Carhart McGill and Associates."

"It ended." She crossed her arms over her chest. "You're investigating them?" Good lord, how crooked had Kevin and his father been to attract the notice of the FBI?

Grimes gave her a tight-lipped smile. He was probably in his fifties, short gray hair and a slim build. The look he gave her was decidedly unfriendly. "Is there someplace quiet we can go to talk? I have a couple of questions."

Uneasiness slithered through her belly. It would be just like Kevin to try to implicate her to cover up his own guilt. And was it a crime that she hadn't reported her suspicions to the police? "If you give me your card we can set up an appointment. I think I'd like to speak with an attorney before talking with the FBI."

"It won't take long." He pushed his suit jacket back to rest his hands on his hips, exposing the gun at his waist in the process. "Just a friendly conversation, no need to get lawyers involved."

She snorted. She was definitely getting lawyers involved now. Frantic waving caught her attention from the corner of her eye. Patty. "I have to go." Kevin was on his feet now, his hand at the back of Patty's neck.

The FBI agent stepped in front of her. "Ms. Sullivan, I don't think you understand the seriousness of the situation."

Patty jerked away from Kevin, fear on her face. "I understand it just fine. Talk to my attorney." She ignored the fact that she didn't have one yet. Or didn't know if she could even afford one. She skirted around Grimes, but he reached out to grab her arm.

"Ms. Sullivan—"

She had just been practicing the move the day before in her martial arts class with Sam. That could be her only excuse. Instinctively, she whipped her arm around his, bending his wrist in the process to release his grip. She blinked when he squawked in pain. Holy donkey balls, the move had worked. Then realization dawned. "Oh, shit. Are you okay? I didn't mean..."

The agent flexed the fingers of his injured hand. He reached to the back of his waist and pulled out a set of handcuffs.

She stepped back. "I didn't mean to hurt you."

He didn't seem to care. "You're under arrest for assaulting a federal agent." He whipped her around and snapped the first bracelet on.

Henry appeared next to her. "What's going on?"

"I'm being arrested!"

He grimaced. "That's not something I can protect against." He asked to see the agent's badge and took down the number. "Don't talk without a lawyer," he said.

Blood pounded in her ears. She was being arrested. She was going to have a record. Her brother had Olympic medals; she would have a mugshot.

She shook her head. "Help Patty." She jerked her head toward the waitress as the agent started to lead her away. "She's being hassled by her ex."

Henry clenched his fists as he looked between her and Patty.

"You can't do anything for me now." She had to raise her voice to be heard above the din. "Make sure Patty gets back to my house safe. Please."

Henry didn't look happy, but he nodded and turned toward Patty and Kevin.

Bridget caught only a glimpse of her manager's shocked face before she was dragged out the front door.

She was being arrested. She kicked at a bit of gravel as the agent opened the back door to his dark SUV. She hated herself for thinking it. She had so many bigger problems to worry about. But the one thought running through her mind was there was no way Tony would want her back now that she had a record.

Chapter Twenty

"WE HAVE NO CONTACT on the inside." Jake leaned forward, pressing his palms into the rough wooden table in front of him. "All we know is from the eye in the sky."

All they knew wasn't good. Tony ground his teeth. Even at this time of night, sweat trickled down his back from all the gear he was wearing. He was hot, dirty, tired, and couldn't wait to get this mission started.

Delta squad had walked into a trap. A trap that should have been theirs.

"They're being held in this corner room." Jake turned his computer screen around and pointed to the aerial photo. "There's at least ten armed guards walking inside the walls of the compound. Three more on the door of the room our brothers are being held. Their mission was to rescue a geneticist who this organization had kidnapped.

We now know said geneticist never existed. It was a set-up from start to finish."

Ryan cracked the knuckles on his right hand. "Are they asking for a ransom?"

"Prisoner exchange." Jake looked each of them in the eye. "They want Omer Abdi back."

Chris barked out a laugh. "Don't they know our government doesn't consider any of our lives worth that dirtbag's? They wouldn't trade our whole battalion for that man."

"Yeah, they should have taken some minor celebrity instead." Travis checked the slide of his sidearm. "They would have had more success."

"None of that matters." Jake closed the computer and slid into his tactical vest. "We're going in and getting our men out. Any enemy casualties along the way are a bonus."

They went over their plan two more times. Horses would get them close but the actual entry would be done on foot.

Tony rechecked his med bag. He didn't know what type of injuries his fellow Raiders might have, but chances were they were severe. The infrared shots from their drone showed two figures in the cell unmoving on the floor.

Another image clawed into his brain. One of Bridget, unmoving. He'd left her with the best protection he could get on short notice, but he should have been the one watching her back. He tightened the strap on his M4, and looped it over his head.

Jake came to his side. "Where are you at?" he asked quietly.

Tony shook his head, confused.

"You distracted?" Jake arched an eyebrow. "Thinking about something other than our mission here?"

Tony dropped his head back on his shoulders and stared at the low ceiling. The abandoned farmhouse they'd occupied had enough land surrounding it to land an evac chopper, but its quarters were too tight. Stifling. It made him twitchy.

"I am thinking about her, but I'll put it away." Tony inhaled sharply. "I'll do my job. We'll get them out. Besides"—he lifted one shoulder and prayed with everything he had that his next words were true—"it's probably nothing. Just some asshole playing a prank on her."

Jake leaned close, his light green eyes glowing in the dim light. "It could be nothing. It could be the biggest fucking thing in the world. Doesn't matter. You did what you could for her at home, now you have to push it out of your head completely. You can't do anything more for her now, but we need you here one hundred percent."

He was right. Tony had to let that part of him go while he was here. His entire focus had to be on the mission or else he and his friends might not make it back home. He nodded once. "You have my one hundred percent."

"Good." Jake stepped back. "Hawk, after the rescue, as soon as we've cleared the compounds walls, I want a message sent out for the evac to get in the air."

Ryan nodded. "It will be waiting for us."

"Trip, you take point on any noncombatants we encounter." Jake rested his hands on his hips. "You're the only one whose French is worth a damn."

"Por supuesto." Chris grinned.

"Moron," Travis muttered. He straightened as Jake addressed him.

"One Shot, don't let any concerns about our last op fuck with your head now." Jake gripped his shoulder. "Take any shot you feel is warranted. We're getting Delta back, even if we have to burn the whole compound down."

"Oorah," Travis agreed.

Jake slid his Ka-bar into his vest. "And Viper, we won't have much time for patching our guys up on site. It's a plug-and-go operation. Understood?"

"Understood." Tony only hoped there was something left to plug. Terrorists weren't known for their mercy.

But then, neither were they.

They all checked their gear one more time and headed out to the corral. A certain stillness came with the night. As if the world itself was holding its breath in anticipation.

Tony swung onto his horse. Chris held the line for the five horses they were taking with them, each wearing an empty saddle. In a couple of hours they wouldn't be empty. They'd be carrying their fellow Raiders. Their friends. Their family.

At a nod, they followed Psych. They were trained in rescue. They were trained in killing. They would get Delta back.

There was no other option.

Chapter Twenty-One

"WELL, THAT WAS A new experience for me." Sam slid her sunglasses from the top of her head to cover her eyes. "I've never bailed anyone out of jail before."

Bridget stood for a moment on the top of the county jail's steps. She'd never appreciated just how sweet fresh air smelled. How good the sun felt on her skin. Spending a night in the pokey was something she never wanted to experience again. "I can't thank you enough. I really didn't want to have to call my parents. I'm already the black sheep of the family. Being arrested would have just been another humiliation."

Sam led her to her Honda Civic. "You were an IT Manager at a large firm and now successfully run a bar. How is that black sheep material?"

Bridget didn't know yet how successfully she was running the *Ginger*. Time would tell. But she appreciated her friend's support. "Athletics are everything to my family. You know about their medals. It was a huge disappointment to my parents when I came out of the womb as uncoordinated as a baby giraffe and stayed that way. Especially with my height. My mom so wanted me to become the gymnast she couldn't be, but I kept falling off the balance beam."

Sam started the car. "Being uncoordinated isn't black sheep material."

"Maybe not." But it sure felt like it. She always seemed to fail to meet the expectations of the people she loved. She fiddled with the hem of her T-shirt. "Have you heard anything? About the guys?"

Sam's fingers tightened on the wheel. "No. And we won't. Not until they get home. The not knowing is just something you have to learn to live with."

"No, I don't." She looked out the window as Jacksonville came into sight. "Tony and I are done."

"Uh huh." Sam didn't sound convinced. "I think Tony knows a criminal attorney. You might want to ask him to hook you up when he gets back."

Tony probably did. She probably wore Armani suits and had perfect hair and make-up. "I don't think that will be necessary. The public defender I talked to said he thinks the charges will be dropped. The fed was trying to use the threat of a conviction to get me to turn evidence on Kevin and his father. I was happy to tell them everything I know about their books. I didn't need coercion." Apparently Kevin Senior's executive assistant had been the one to take the external hard drive. After helping the Carharts in their dirty dealings for a couple of years, she'd grown a conscience and taken evidence to the SEC.

Kevin and his father were the ones who were going to need lawyers. Good ones. A twinge of sorrow touched her heart at the thought that the man she once thought she'd marry might go to prison. But he'd made his choices. He'd have to live with them.

Just like she had to live with hers.

Sam turned into the parking lot of the *Ginger*. It was Monday, the day they were closed, so Gimli should have been the only car there, but two other were parked near the front door.

"Hey, your car looks all shiny. New paint?" Sam asked as she pulled alongside.

"Tony did it after someone scratched it up." Gimli really did look handsome without the rust and dents. Tony hated her car, but he'd spent his time, and money, to make it look as good as it possibly could. For her.

She rubbed her breastbone. While they'd been together, he'd always put her first. Treated her right. Had she overreacted? After all, she didn't think he was perfect. Why did she expect him to think she was? If she could love him despite his pressed shirts, his insistence on waking up at ungodly hours to go workout, and his complete lack of knowledge of role playing games, then couldn't he love her, too?

The driver's side and passenger doors on one of the cars by the *Ginger* both popped open, and two familiar figures stepped out.

"What are Caroline and Willow doing here?" Bridget asked.

"Yeah, about that." Sam put her car into park. She shot Bridget a guilty look. "Caroline's kitchen is being remodeled and the workmen are making a lot of noise. Willow's jam shop is hosting a small private event for one of her daughter's teachers, and my place is just too small. I suggested that maybe we could do some wedding planning here? Where there's drinks and maybe some chips and queso?"

Bridget arched an eyebrow.

Sam pressed her hands together in a prayer pose. "I know it was awfully presumptuous of me, but I did think there might be some perks to bailing you out?"

Bridget snorted. She owed Sam a lot more than some table space and snacks. "Let's go."

As they walked to the front door, Sam held out a key. "Karen gave me her key to the *Ginger* to give to you. And she said your purse is in one of your desk drawers."

"Thanks." She greeted the other women, and they made their way inside. Bridget flipped on the lights and went behind the bar. "What does everyone want?"

"Diet soda for me." Caroline pulled a huge binder from a backpack she carried. "I have to fit into my dress."

"Yeah, like that will be a problem." Willow eyed her friend. "You don't have to worry about your weight for this wedding."

Caroline slumped into a wooden chair. "No, just everything else is a problem. Why are weddings this complicated? And expensive."

"Mine wasn't." Willow took a chip from the bowl Bridget set down in the center of the table. "Me and Bill just went to the justice of the peace and then took some friends and family to a restaurant. Of course, I was four months pregnant with Matilda at the time. Our situation was different."

"But if you and Travis get married, I bet you'll go big with that wedding." Sam pulled a folder from Caroline's binder and pulled out some papers. "Ooh, salmon canapes. Fancy."

"Look at the number at the bottom of that catering bid." Caroline shook her head. "I don't think we're doing salmon."

Bridget sat back and enjoyed just listening to her new friends plan. These were good problems to discuss. Happy problems, if such a thing existed. It helped take her mind off her own, not so fun, issues. She shoveled a tortilla chip into the bowl of salsa. She'd missed chips and salsa during her time in the slammer. It had only been eighteen hours, but it had felt much longer. She was so happy to be free, she didn't even mind the glop of salsa that landed on her shirt.

"Did you decide where you're going to have the reception?" Willow asked.

"We'd been thinking the Rangewood Golf and Country Club, but now I don't know." Caroline pulled a glossy brochure from her binder and stared at it glumly. "It's pretty, but a bit stuffy. And we don't even play golf."

"Well, if everything goes tits up, you can always hold it here," Bridget joked.

"The chips and salsa are good." Sam grinned.

Caroline planted her elbow on the table and dropped her chin into her upraised palm. "Realistically, where doesn't matter. I'm just nervous. Jake left with one of his feelings. I'm worried we might not have this wedding at all. What if something goes wrong on this mission?"

"You can't think that way." Sam tugged on Caroline's pale ponytail. "The guys are seriously well-trained. And Jake knows he has you waiting for him. He'll be fine."

Bridget laid her latest chip on her napkin, no longer hungry. Dear God, these women had to face this fear every time the men left on a mission. Her stomach churned. Tony had left right after they'd fought. He left not thinking she was waiting for him.

She stood. "I'm going to be in my office doing a bit of work. Feel free to go behind the bar and get refills whenever you want."

She researched a new inventory system while the women discussed flowers and bands. After two hours, they were all ready to call it quits.

"Thanks for letting us hang out here," Caroline said, shrugging into her jacket.

"Any time." Bridget locked up after them, forcing a smile. When would Tony and the rest of them get home? Yes, she'd said she hadn't wanted to see him again, but she needed to know he was safe.

Sam tooted her horn in farewell as Bridget got in her car.

Bridget drove home on autopilot. Her mind was too overloaded worrying about a hundred different things so she just let it drift. Patty's car was in front of the porch steps, and Bridget parked hers under the carport.

She kicked off her shoes when she entered. "Hi Patty."

Patty sat up from her sprawl on the sofa and turned off the TV. "I hope you don't mind. Karen found your spare keys in the office and gave them to me."

"Of course, I don't mind. I invited you." She looked toward the kitchen where she knew a cold beer waited for her in the fridge. But a shower was first priority. She headed for the stairs. "Any problems with Matt after I...left?" She didn't want to say arrested.

"No, some military guy came over and told him to leave." A small smile crossed her face. "It was an order Matt couldn't refuse. You should have seen the muscles on this guy."

Bridget had seen them. They were nice, but they didn't compare to the muscles she wanted wrapped around her, holding her tight right now.

Patty stopped her when she had one foot on the first step. "Oh, um, last night, I heard some things." The woman rubbed her palms up and down her thighs. "Strange noises. Is that usual?"

"Just my ghost." She really needed to call an exterminator. She almost wished it was Kieran's spirit. Maybe then she wouldn't feel so alone.

Patty flopped back on the sofa. "Thank God. Ghosts I can handle. I thought you had a rat infestation."

Bridget kept her mouth shut. She was halfway up the stairs when she paused. She looked at the ceiling where she had seen her 'ghostly' lights. They had been explained away the night Tony had peered through her window with a flashlight. But what about the other time she'd seen them? Had someone been outside her house then, as well?

She pursed her lips and slowly made her way to her room and the shower. After scrubbing the feeling of jail from her body, she found one of Tony's T-shirts he had forgotten at her house and slipped it on. When he got back, she'd have another talk with him. A real one, where she laid it all out. Her hopes. Her fears. Her love. It could work out between them. She could give a little; he could give a little.

She flopped onto the bed and stared at the ceiling.

She only hoped she wasn't fooling herself.

Chapter Twenty-Two

THE BACK OF HIS throat felt as gritty as his eyes. Tony parked in the corner of the *Ginger's* lot and stared up at the steel-gray sky. He didn't see the lightning, but thunder rumbled overhead, evidence of its presence.

It had been bad. Worse than anything he'd yet to encounter in his time with the Raiders. One man from Delta dead. One seriously injured. The rest of the squad had minor injuries, but when Tony had looked into their eyes, he knew their wounds ran deep.

A friend, a brother, dead. And Nathan would never be the same. His military career was over, that was for certain. The hospitals were coming out with better prosthetics every year, but they weren't good enough to keep a man on special forces active duty.

And it should have been Alpha walking into that trap.

He pulled out his phone and texted his friend that he was here. Then he got out and waited for him outside the front door. "McAvoy." They shook hands.

"How bad?" McAvoy asked.

Tony relayed what details he could. "As squad leader, Redwood is feeling responsible. I could see the guilt in his eyes. He's going to need our support. They all will."

McAvoy nodded, his jaw clenched. "Did you make them pay?"

Tony clenched his jaw. "Yeah. They paid all right."

McAvoy squeezed his shoulder. "Well, everything's fine on the home front. There was a situation with law enforcement the other night, but I'll let your girl tell you about that."

His girl. Right now, Tony didn't care if Bridget told him she'd been arrested for mooning the mayor. If she would agree to be his girl, they could work anything else out.

He caught sight of her right when he entered the bar. How could he not? With her beautiful hair, luminous skin, and welcoming laugh, she stood out as if there was a spotlight on her. It took him a couple of seconds of just drinking the sight of her in before he noticed the dress.

Knee length, dark blue, and tucked in at the waist. It was feminine, demure, and so very unlike Bridget he rubbed his eyes, wondering if he'd reached the point of exhaustion where he was hallucinating.

He threaded his way through the early evening crowd until he stood right behind her, breathing in her honey-suckle scent.

She turned without him saying anything, her eyes widening when she saw him. She swallowed. "You're okay?"

He nodded. 'Okay' was relative. He was as good as could be under the circumstances.

He'd be better if Bridget was in his arms. But he hesitated. They hadn't left it on the best of terms. He might have his work cut out for him before he could hold her again.

He fingered the tiny bow on her collar. "Why the dress?"

She smoothed her hand down her abdomen. "I wanted to try dressing like an adult." Her mouth twisted. "The heels only lasted an hour. My feet were killing me. Thankfully I had a pair of these in the office I could change into." She pointed her toe, showing off the canvas sneakers.

"You look beautiful," he told her honestly. "You look just as good in jeans and a T-shirt."

"Really?" The hopeful look on her face slayed him. He'd done that to her. Put that doubt in her head that she was less somehow because she wasn't his usual type. And why wouldn't she feel that way? He hadn't treated this as a real relationship. That was changing now.

"There's someone I want you to meet." He always called Eloise when he came back from a mission. He could kill two birds with one stone. Introducing Bridget to Elle would have to show her that he was serious. That he wanted them to be serious.

Bridget scraped her teeth over her bottom lip. "Uh, okay. But can we—" The ringing of the phone in her hand interrupted her. She frowned down at the screen that showed a number with a local area code. "That might be the exterminator," she muttered. "Hold that thought."

"Hello." Her face drew into a frown. "Kevin, why are you calling me? I don't think I'm supposed to be talking to you."

She covered her ear with one hand, turning her back to the bar crowd. "No, I won't say that to the investigators. I already talked to the FBI. I told them what I knew."

A torrent of curses and threats came from her phone. Tony held out his hand. "Give me the phone." He'd need Bridget to give him a sitrep, tell him just what the hell had happened since he'd been gone, but no way was he going to let any man talk to her that way.

Her eyebrows drew closer. She took a step away. "You can go self-pleasure yourself, too. And with a rusty implement. I'm not going to lie for you." *No swearing for two days*, she mouthed to Tony with a thumbs-up. "Now you're just being rude," she said back into the phone. She slapped at Tony's hand when he tried to take it away from her.

"Hi Tony." A tall woman in a silk wrap-dress pressed against his side.

He only gave her half his attention. "Melissa. How are you doing?" Bridget was still arguing into the phone when she should have just hung up, or better yet, given him the phone, but she gave him the stink eye as she talked.

"I'm here with some girlfriends and saw you come in." Melissa shook her blond hair off her shoulder. "I was just remembering what a good time we had together."

"Uh huh." Why was Bridget looking at him like that? He wasn't the asshole screaming in her ear.

"I was thinking we should try it again? I know you hang out here, so I was hoping we could talk." Melissa's voice was an annoying buzz in his ear. He gave Bridget the wrap it up hand signal, but she just glared.

He followed her narrowed gaze to his arm. And the finger Melissa was trailing up his sleeve.

"What do you say? This Friday?" Melissa gave him an inviting grin, one that offered everything he didn't want.

Gently, he removed her hand. "Sorry. I'm with her." He pointed at the place Bridget had been standing. His back tensed as he looked around the bar. No flash of red hair. No wide-set whiskey eyes. "Where'd she go?"

"Who?"

"Have a good evening, Melissa, but I'm taken." And he set off to track down the woman who had taken every part of him. She couldn't think that the person he wanted her to meet was Melissa, could she? He trotted to the back office. Empty. Poked his head in the kitchen. No Bridget. It would be just his damn luck if Bridget misinterpreted what she saw just as Tony was finally getting his head on straight.

He waited outside the women's restroom until a middle-aged lady came out. "Excuse me, is there anyone else in there?" he asked.

She looked a little startled but replied, "No, it was just me."

Tony pulled out his phone and called Bridget. No answer. He cursed. She couldn't have been so angry with him that she'd left. But just in case, he checked the parking lot. Gimli was still there.

He cracked his neck. People didn't just disappear from well-lit bars. A few drops of rain fell on his head, and he stepped back inside. He pulled over a waitress who was walking past. "I need to find Bridget."

"She was just...." The woman rolled onto her toes and scanned the bar. "Huh. I'll ask some of the others if they've seen her."

But no one had. Tony tried calling her again. No answer.

After a minute more of searching every closet and back room, Marcus lumbered up to him, wiping his hands on his apron. "Come with me."

Tony followed him out the back and into the alleyway.

"Call Bridget again," Marcus said. He went to the open dumpster and peered down. After a few seconds, a ringtone sounded from the dumpster.

Tony lowered his hand. "What?" His heart beat triple time.

"I heard it ringing when I was taking out the trash, then I heard you were looking for Bridget." Marcus scrubbed his hand across his jaw. "I think its hers. Someone dumped her phone."

The other part of that sentence went unsaid. If someone had dumped her phone, that someone had also taken Bridget.

Tony sprinted to the end of the alley and peered down the empty street. His breath came out in short gasps.

She was gone.

Chapter Twenty-Three

BRIDGET'S HAND TWITCHED, BRINGING awareness to that part of her body. The next thing her brain recognized was that it was dark where she was. Had a noise woken her? She tried to sit up, and smacked her head on something metal looming above her.

"What the...?" She lay back down, and something hard poked into her spine. Her breaths were hard, heavy, but she could barely hear them over the drone of an engine.

She was in a car. A trunk, more specifically. And she couldn't remember how she'd gotten there.

She tried to stifle the rising panic. She'd been annoyed with Kevin. Annoyed with that skank hanging all over Tony. So she'd hung up on her ex mid-sentence and headed into the kitchen for a slice of their peanut butter chocolate cake.

She rubbed her forehead. There'd been garbage stacked by the door. Before getting her cake, she'd taken it out to the dumpster. And then....

Then she was here. Shoved in the trunk of a car.

She should have had the piece of cake first.

Knowing it was useless, she couldn't stop her instinct to pound on the ceiling of the trunk. "Help! Someone help me!"

Only the sound of the road answered.

She closed her eyes, trying to fight the sting of tears. Screaming wasn't going to cut it. She had to think. Carefully rolling to her side, she felt around the compartment. Scratchy fabric. Smooth rubber.

Cold metal.

She clutched the slim bar and felt along its edges. It was one of those x-shaped tire irons, not ideal for getting in a good swing, but it would have to do.

She tensed when the car turned from smooth pavement to a bumpy road. Clutching the tire iron to her chest, she shifted her weight, trying to get into the best position for leaping out of the trunk. Her breaths came in choppy pants. Her palms grew slick.

She wouldn't freeze up. She wouldn't let herself.

The car rolled to a stop. A door opened. Closed.

When that trunk opened, she would be moving. There was no room for fear. She visualized her prison door opening, her jumping out and swinging for the fences, the faceless kidnapper falling unconscious at her feet. She could do this. She could....

The trunk door popped open. She forced her cramped muscles to move. But her body didn't work as she'd visualized. Instead of the graceful leap out, her knee caught the lip of the trunk and she tumbled forward, the ground rushing up to meet her.

She rolled to her feet and came up swinging. And hit nothing but air.

Matt Dunkel stood a safe distance away from her arm reach. A baseball hat shielded his face from the fat raindrops that dripped from the darkening sky. "You like games?" He raised his hand, dark metal in his grasp. "Gun beats stick, every time. Drop it."

It was the hardest thing to do, dropping that tire iron. Without is, she felt completely exposed. It hadn't been much of a weapon, but it had been something. "What are you doing?"

"Showing her that I'm serious." He jerked the gun, indicating she should move, and she finally noticed where she was. Kieran's house. The porch light shone dimly in the gathering twilight. "Inside," he said.

Bridget didn't know if she was more confused or scared. The barrel of the gun jabbed into her back when she stumbled up the porch stairs, and her heart beat triple time.

Definitely more scared. "You vandalized my car."

He didn't answer.

She pulled open her front door. "Did you start the fire here, too?"

"I've done more than you know." He shoved her across the threshold and followed her inside. He turned and pointed a finger at Patty, who sat gaping on the sofa. "All to prove my love to her."

"What's going on?" Patty stood. She wore a tank top and pajama shorts, looking like she had settled in for an early evening. "Is that a gun?"

"Of course, it's a gun." Matt waved it in the air. "You always ask dumb questions."

Bridget pressed her back against the wall. She took half a step toward the kitchen. There were lots of things in a kitchen that made good weapons. "That doesn't sound like love to me. It sounds like you're a condescending prick."

Matt swung the gun in her direction, and she froze. "What do you know about love? You spread your legs for a guy who's always got his eye out for something better."

Bridget clenched her fists. Okay, that...cut a little too close to home. But for this asshole to know that was her fear, he must have been watching her more closely than she'd thought.

"But Matt...." Patty pressed her palms to her abdomen. "What do you think this will get you? I can't control who I love, and kidnapping Bridget will only land you in jail."

Matt closed the distance between them and cupped her cheek. It would have looked almost sweet if the muzzle of his gun wasn't pressing into her side. "I just need you back home with me. Once you're there, you'll see. You do love me. You need me. She's in our way, but once she's gone, you'll come back to me."

Bridget's legs felt as weak as her punches, but she forced them to inch toward the kitchen. It really didn't sound like she had a happy ending in Matt's plans. She tried to slow her breathing and think. There were dozens of sharp, pointy things in the kitchen. And the granite mortar. Or was it a pestle? Whatever. She could brain him with it, regardless of its name. She just had to get to the kitchen, pick out a weapon, and then—

"Stop moving!" Matt's hand shook as he pointed the gun at her. Sweat beaded on his temple. This guy wasn't playing with a full fifty-two card deck, and that knowledge scared Bridget more than anything.

"Matt, don't." It was a valiant effort, but even Bridget could see how weak Patty's attempt to grab the gun was.

Matt shrugged her off, cuffing her with the back of her hand. He glared down at her, sprawled at his feet. "You'd take her side?" He made an odd noise in the back of his throat, somewhere between a growl and a whine. "You don't return my calls, my texts, my messages. You try to cut me out of your life. And even after I show you my love again and again, you stand against me?"

Bridget darted for the kitchen door. The wall in front of her exploded, bits of plaster and wood from the hole the bullet made biting her skin like insects. She skidded to a stop, her feet going out from under her. Her dress swirled around her hips as her butt hit the floor.

"Don't move!" Matt shouted. "This is your fault. Yours and your uncle's. He would never fire her, not even with all the times she was late or missed work. If he would have only fired her, she would have had to come back to me."

Bridget's heartbeat slowed. The pulsing of the blood in her ears sounded sluggish. "Her flat tire. All those problems with Patty's apartments. The floods, the power outage. you created them to try to get her to move back in with you. You want her dependent on you."

"She just needs to realize how much she needs me." He bent over and shouted in Patty's face, "You need me!"

"My uncle." The words tasted like ash on her tongue. Kieran had been a good man. He'd tried to help Patty.

"I didn't know the fall would kill him. I wanted him to know how serious I was." Matt shrugged. "He fell wrong."

Bridget was too stunned to move, even if Matt hadn't kept the gun pointed in her direction. He'd said it so casually. Like killing her uncle was of no more importance than swatting a bug.

Matt yanked on the cord to the curtains. He pulled the thin strings free as one side of the curtain rod fell to the sofa. He tossed the strings to Patty. "Tie her hands behind her back. Get on your stomach," he said to Bridget.

She looked at his gun. Looked at the distance to the kitchen. The front door. Any exit. She wouldn't make it. She went to her stomach.

The strings bit into her skin. They were thin, but wrapped around her wrists several times, they were too strong for Bridget to pull apart. She awkwardly rolled to sitting as Matt grabbed Patty's arm. "Let's go," he said.

Patty shook free and wiped at her wet cheeks. "I'm not going anywhere with you. I hate you!"

Bridget could have told her that was the wrong play. The woman should have played nice with the crazy man, told him what he wanted to hear. She'd live longer. Long enough to attempt an escape. The punch that Matt landed on the waitress's face didn't come as a surprise.

"After everything I've done for you." He kicked Patty's fallen form. "Everything I gave you." He grabbed her hair, yanking her head back, and put his face close to hers. "You don't appreciate any of it. Don't appreciate me. I'm done with you. You'd rather stay with this bitch, here? That's fine. You can die with her, too."

He rained blows on Patty. Most of them hit her upraised arms, but a few got through. The sound of Patty's head hitting the hard wood floor was one Bridget would never forget. Bridget screamed at him to stop. Patty screamed. But he hit her until Patty stopped moving.

Matt panted, staring down at his ex-girlfriend's body. His chin wobbled, like he might actually feel some regret.

But then he turned and looked at Bridget, and she knew. He didn't feel regret. He wasn't capable of it.

He'd killed her uncle. And now he was going to kill her, too.

Chapter
Twenty-Four

Tony checked the last window. Locked, like every other entry into the small home. He pressed his phone between his shoulder and chin as he pulled his kit from his rear pocket. "I told you, it was a local area code he called from. There has to be a plane ticket. Gas receipts. Something to show he travelled from California to here."

"I've looked." Ryan murmured something to someone next to him. He came back on the line. "As far as I can tell, Bridget's ex hasn't left California."

"Then how—"

"He could have been using a burner number." The sound of a keyboard clacking came over the phone line. Ryan wouldn't stop checking, no matter what he told Tony. "Sales people use local area codes to try to get you to pick up their call."

The tumbler in the back door's lock slipped back into place. Tony cursed. Picking a lock while holding a conversation wasn't easy. Rain plinked off the tin roof of the porch.

"I'm putting you on speaker," Ryan said.

"Viper." Jake's voice was a warning. "Where are you right now? You can't do anything stupid."

Tony rested his forehead against the door jamb. He knew he couldn't afford stupid. Not if he wanted to get Bridget back. He hadn't even waited for the cops to arrive after Karen called them. He'd left the manager the security footage showing an unidentifiable figure grabbing Bridget by the dumpsters, then gotten in his car and called Ryan, their computer guru. It had been only a matter of moments for Ryan to come up with the name and address of the waitress's ex, the only other suspect Tony had.

"What about cars leaving the area?" Shoving his lockpick kit away in frustration, he took two steps back from the door. "He couldn't have carried Bridget far. There have to be other cameras that caught him." He planted his boot on the section of door by its lock and watched with satisfaction as it burst open. If the guy was innocent, Tony would buy him a new door.

"I'm working on it," Ryan said evenly.

Tony knew his friend only had two hands, and he was asking Ryan to check everything at once. He was lucky Ryan hadn't blown his lid at him yet. But he was too scared to think rationally. Bridget was gone. Taken. And he needed to get her back.

"What was that sound?" Jake asked. "It sounded like a door."

Tony didn't respond. He swung his penlight over the darkened interior. Matt Dunkel was a slob. It was no wonder his girlfriend had left him.

Jake sighed over the line. "Are you wearing gloves?"

"No." And Tony didn't care if he left prints. Nothing mattered unless he found Bridget.

"I'm sending Travis and Chris to your location," Jake said. "Wait for them."

"It's not Bridget's ex." Ryan's voice was grim.

"What?" Tony went to the kitchen. Scanned the assortment of magnets on the fridge. The line of ants marching to a chipped butter dish.

"Kevin Carhart," Ryan said. "He didn't take Bridget. I found him. He's in police custody in California. Was just picked up twenty minutes ago."

Tony closed his eyes. After that call Bridget had got, he had really thought her ex was the one who'd taken her. Lured her outside with the call. Having her ex removed as a suspect felt like the rug had just been pulled beneath his feet.

"We'll get her back." Their squad leader's voice was confident. "Ryan will work more of his magic and find the cars leaving the area in the timeframe you gave us. We'll filter them down and find her."

Tony's stomach hardened. He moved down the hallway, peeking in at a bedroom. A bathroom. Yes, they'd find her. But a lot could happen to Bridget between now and then. He had to tell her what an ass he'd been. Tell her how much he loved her. Needed her.

His feet froze on the threshold of a guest bedroom. Dunkel had turned it into an office of sorts. "Find out what kind of car Matt Dunkel drives. I need a location on it now."

"I've already been looking for it." Ryan sounded offended. "But we need to look at all the options. It could have been—"

"It's him." His light swept over picture after picture taped to the walls. Most were of Patty, obviously taken when she wasn't looking. But it was the photos with large, red Xs drawn through them that sent ice to his veins.

"He has pictures of Bridget in his house." So many pictures. He pulled one off the wall. It was of him and Bridget. They had been walking to a restaurant downtown. Their second date, if Tony remembered correctly. Even then, the look on his face when he stared down at Bridget showed everything he'd felt. He'd been head over heels with her that early on. He'd just been too stupid to realize it.

He couldn't see Bridget's expression. The red marker sliced through her face like a blade.

The picture crumpled in Tony's fist. "Ryan. Please." He cleared his throat. He just had to hold it together a bit longer. Until he found Bridget. There had been too much death recently. Too much hurt. He didn't know if he'd survive if something happened to Bridget, too. "Find that car."

"I will," his friend promised. "Don't worry. We're going to get her back."

Tony nodded, even though they couldn't see him. He believed Ryan. His friends had made Bridget their mission now, and they never failed in a mission.

But finding Bridget wasn't nearly as important as *how* they found her. And if that asshole had hurt one hair on her head, Tony was going to rip him apart, piece by piece.

Chapter Twenty-Five

PATTY SUCKED AT TYING knots. Which might be the only thing that could save their lives. The scratching noises had stopped, and the only sound that came from outside was the patter of rain against the roof. Matt had disappeared outside after tying Patty up, and the silence from him now was almost scarier than his rages.

"I can't believe he killed Kieran." Patty tucked her knees to her chest, somehow making the position look graceful even with her arms tied behind her back, too.

"I've almost got it." Bridget rubbed the knot over the exposed hinge of the closet door. She couldn't think about her uncle now. If the enormity of what had been taken from her family hit her, she wouldn't be able to function.

"I knew he could fly into rages, but I never imagined...." Patty rested her cheek on her knee. "I just can't believe it."

"Uh huh." Another strand loosened. Bridget's shoulders ached from their awkward position, and she didn't hold out much hope that she still had any skin on her wrists, but she wasn't going to let this bastard take her life like he had her uncle's. Not without one hell of a fight.

Something slopped against the outside wall, and Bridget froze. "What was that?"

"Sounds like something spilled." A furrow creased Patty's forehead.

The sound repeated. And again.

"Oh God," Bridget breathed as the scent reached her nose. She redoubled her effort on her ties, her bound hands pumping up and down. "It's gasoline. He's pouring gas around the house."

"He wouldn't...."

Bridget glared at Patty. How much more evidence did the woman need to see that her ex was a psychopath?

Her hands snapped free so suddenly it caught her off guard. "I'm free." She shook out her hands. They were numb and tingling in places, but she couldn't wait for the blood to return. She opened the closet door and grabbed her sword with two hands. "Turn around."

Patty's eyes flew wide, but she scooted around on her butt until her bound hands were facing Bridget. Matt was much better at tying knots than Patty, but Bridget kept her sword sharp. *And sword beats rope, asshole.*

"Let's go." Bridget ignored the small cuts she'd given Patty and stood on wobbling feet. Patty leaned against the wall, her face a patchwork of bruises, her hand pressed to her ribs. Matt had taken Patty's cell phone, but Kieran had a landline. She only hoped the cops and firemen could reach them before they, and the house, were destroyed.

The screen on the kitchen door squealed, and she and Patty froze. Bridget adjusted her grip on the hilt and tried to channel her inner warrior. She could do this. Man had been running each other through with swords for thousands of years. It was only the last century or two that they'd become squeamish about it.

She visualized a parry. A thrust. And almost lost her lunch at the vivid image that swept through her mind of the tip of her sword piercing flesh. The blood. The torn flesh. Damn her imagination.

Her moment of weakness cost her. When Matt came around the corner, she hesitated.

He didn't. He took in their new position in an instant, lowered his shoulder, and charged. He caught her under the ribs, tossing her back like a lineman would a rookie quarterback. She just missed the coffee table, and her sword skittered away on the hardwood floor.

With a shriek Bridget hadn't thought Patty capable of, the woman launched herself at her ex, jumping on his back and wrapping herself around him like a kudzu vine. Matt peeled Patty off of him, limb by limb, grabbed her by the nape of her neck, and smashed her head into the nearest wall.

She dropped, unmoving.

Bridget scrambled on her knees and belly. She grabbed her sword, got on one knee, and spun around just as Matt reached into the back of his pants and pulled his gun out.

She sliced at his wrist, and he dropped the weapon with a yowl. Blood dripped from the shallow cut, and Matt cradled his hand to his abdomen. "You bitch. I would have loved her forever if you hadn't gotten in the way. This is your fault."

Bridget had no words. So she raised the hilt to her shoulder, aimed her sword at his heart, and charged.

She was almost relieved when he turned tail and ran before she could stab him. It was the mess, she told herself as she chased him into the kitchen. She didn't want to have to clean up the mess she'd make killing a man. If he kept running, she'd be happy to leave him for the police.

But he didn't keep running. He made it to the back porch where he turned and waited for her, chest heaving.

"If you'd only let her go, none of this would have happened," he said.

Bridget stepped out on the porch, the screen swinging shut behind her. The porch wasn't an ideal location to attack someone with a sword. The ceiling was a bit too low. The area not quite wide enough for a full swing. But the narrow space would make it easier to keep him in front of her. "I can say the same thing about you." She took a step forward, jabbing at him, making him retreat.

He reached into his front pants pocket. The object was too small to be a weapon, but still Bridget tensed. She jabbed at him again, and he took another step back, reaching the corner of the porch. Then he smiled.

That smile froze her blood.

He held up the small object, and flicked his thumb. A flame burst to life.

Bridget was too terrified to even swear. The porch was drenched in gasoline. The smell was already giving her a headache. She stood in a puddle of the flammable liquid. She tried to swallow, but had no spit. This was very, very bad.

A gentle breeze caressed her cheek like a touch.

And the flame went out.

Matt lit it again.

The flame sputtered out again.

Bridget barked out a short laugh. "Kind of ironic. You've used gallons of fuel all around the house but your lighter is empty." She must be going into shock. For some reason she felt calm again. Safe even. Like she wasn't alone.

He shook the red plastic tube. "There's still some in there," he muttered.

Matt got a flame after several more attempts, and smiled. The wind picked up. The porch creaked. And suddenly he was moving, stumbling forward, the lighter leaving his hand and sailing over the railing into the backyard.

Bridget tried to get out of the way. She stepped to the side but it wasn't enough. Matt fell on the point of her sword.

It impaled him a couple of inches below his collar bone, right where Bridget imagined his heart lay. The blade only went in a couple of inches, but it was enough.

Matt gurgled, blinking in surprise, before crumpling to the floor.

Bridget was just as surprised. She'd stabbed a man. Ran him through with her sword. He'd deserved it, yes, but her mind was having a hard time wrapping itself around the enormity of what she'd just done.

As gently as she could, she pulled her sword free. Blood spilled from the wound. Matt's eyes closed.

She pressed the back of her hand to her mouth. Took one deep breath. Two. This was what she'd taken self-defense for. To save her own life and those she cared about, even if it meant taking another's. She had no moral qualms about what she'd done, but she couldn't get her hands to stop shaking.

She tried to pull it together. Channel her inner warrior. "It's not my fault your dead," she told his body, but her voice wobbled just as badly as her knees. She laid her sword on the porch railing and bent in half, trying not to hyperventilate.

If she'd been a true badass, she would have made sure he was dead. She didn't hear him get up. Didn't hear him grab her sword. She only looked up when she heard a shout, one she recognized, one she loved, and saw Tony gripping the porch rail with one hand. He pulled himself up and over in one leap and reached Matt just as the asshole raised the sword like a baseball bat and started to swing for Bridget's head.

One second Matt had a throat. The next it was gone. Tony's three-inch knife blade destroyed it with one quick slash.

Bridget leaped back from the spray of blood. From the sword falling toward her feet. She turned her gaze on the man she loved, thinking that was much nicer to look out than all the horror surrounding her.

Tony stabbed his knife into the porch railing, leaving it sticking up straight. "Now he's dead." Then he stepped over the body and gathered her into his arms.

Bridget burrowed in deep. She didn't care how many differences existed between her and Tony. How many reasons existed why they didn't work.

There was one thing that bonded them together. One thing that gave her the certainty that they could work any other BS out

And that one thing told her to hold on tight to this man and never let him go.

Chapter
Twenty-Six

THE *GINGER* WAS LOUD, even though it was closed. Karen had chosen Monday for the staff party funded by Bridget's swear jar. And the staff of the *Ginger* could party. So much so that they'd even tired his little Irish hellion out. Which suited Tony fine. A tired Bridget wasn't running around having shot drinking contests with her employees. She was where she belonged. With him. And currently that was on his lap at a table surrounded by their friends.

Caroline leaned across the table. "Bridget, were you serious about offering *The Limber Ginger* for our reception?"

Bridget straightened, her bottom rocking against his groin. "Are *you* serious? Of course. I didn't think you'd actually want to have it here."

"It feels wrong to have a big, formal reception with everything that's going on with the squads." Caroline squeezed Jake's leg.

"You know the guys won't begrudge you a wedding." Jake rested his arm on the back of her chair. "We need more happy celebrations."

"And it will be happy." Caroline turned back to Bridget. "This place is almost like a second home to so many of the guys. And I don't want to wait the many months it would take to get everything together for a country club wedding. I want to marry Jake as soon as possible. Life is too short to wait."

Tony couldn't agree with the sentiment more. He squeezed Bridget's hip. They were still new, but he could see their future, and he couldn't wait for it to start.

"Let's get together tomorrow," Bridget said. "We'll work out all the details. Ooh!" She bounced on his lap. "Do you guys do that whole sword arch thing when you get married? 'Cause I could totally get into that."

"It's only Marines who would hold their sabers up," Chris said.

"Hey, my sword has seen actual action and been baptized in blood." Bridget arched an eyebrow. "It should get an honorary spot."

Ryan tossed a nut into the air and caught it in his mouth. "I have to say, of all your assorted women, Viper's scares me the most."

Sam stopped resting her head on Chris's shoulder and sat up straight. "Hey, I resent that."

"Have you ever stabbed someone with a broadsword?" Ryan asked.

Sam slumped back in her chair. "No."

Caroline leaned across Jake and patted her knee.

"Okay, I have to know." Bridget shifted on his lap. "How did Tony get the name Viper?"

The back of his neck heated. "It really isn't—"

"It was six years ago. A desert in some shit country that can't be named." Chris smiled gleefully.

"And I took a leak on a snake," Tony said quickly. "End of story."

Bridget blinked. "You walked up to a viper, unzipped, and peed on it?"

"Yep." Tony looked for a waitress. "Hey, let's order some more—"

"I'm sorry," Travis said. "I can't back that one up. Tell her the truth."

"There were no lies told." Tony glared at his friends.

"But a lot of context was left out," Jake said mildly.

Ryan took up the story. "We were camping and Mr. Prim and Proper didn't want to pee in front of us. So he goes around a rock, unzips, and then starts screaming like a little girl. We grab our weapons and come charging to the rescue only to find that the bathroom he chose was already home to a horned viper."

"He was shouting, 'Shoot it, shoot it,' and dancing around with his pants still unzipped and his...well, you know bouncing around." Chris started laughing. "I'll never get that image out of my head."

Tony ground his teeth. "It leapt at me. Right at my...." He looked at the amusement in all their faces and bit back what he wanted to say. "I don't like snakes, okay?"

Bridget rubbed his arm. "It's all right. You take care of the spiders and I'll handle the snakes."

"Anyway, we thought about calling him Sir Squeals A Lot, but it was a bit too wordy for a call sign." Ryan smirked.

Assholes. His friends were all assholes.

"Hey." Ryan threw a nut at Tony. "Have you gotten the all-clear from the D.A.?"

"Yep." Tony squeezed Bridget's thigh, happy to move on to a different topic. He still couldn't believe how close he'd come to losing her. If he'd been just a second later, if Ryan hadn't seen Dunkel's car on a traffic cam heading toward Bridget's house, he might have lost her. "I have been officially cleared." After everything the police had discovered about Matt Dunkel, there had been no way the D.A. could have justified charging Tony in his death. It would have been political suicide.

Travis ran his fingers through the dark curls spilling down Willow's back. "If you ever want a different job, Bridge, I have some friends in private security. A woman who can take down a man with a sword would be a sought-after commodity."

Tony glared at Travis. "She's not interested." Jesus, he worried about her enough managing this bar. He couldn't take it if she went into security.

Bridget turned on his lap to face him. She gave him a sugary sweet smile. "Sweetie, you know how we talked about your propensity to be overbearing?"

Tony sighed. He was working on it, really, he was. But a man had to set some limits, for his own sanity if nothing else.

She turned back to face the table. "Thanks, but I'm definitely not interested." She scraped her teeth over her bottom lip. "And truth be told, I didn't stab Matt so much as he fell on my sword. It was really strange, the way his lighter kept going out, the way he stumbled forward. It was like he was pushed. At first I thought Patty had come around the side porch and shoved him, but she was still unconscious when we went to check on her."

"People stumble over their own feet all the time." Travis shrugged. "And frequently, it saves lives. Just ask Trip how *he* got his call sign." He nodded at Chris.

"Asshole, I didn't fall!" Chris glowered.

Sam rubbed his chest soothingly.

"What do you think happened?" Jake brought a long-neck to his mouth and took a sip, his gaze steady on Bridget.

Tony felt her tense. He knew what she thought. He also knew it was crazy. But crazy shit did happen. He and Bridget were proof of that.

Bridget scraped at the label on her bottle of lager. "You'll think I'm nuts, but I felt something there. A presence. After the police found evidence that Dunkel had been hanging around my attic and crawl space spying on me, I know there were rational explanations for every time I saw lights or heard noises, but I can't help but think that Uncle Kieran was there that night, watching over me."

The table went silent. Tony gave each of his friend's a hard stare, daring them to say Bridget was talking nonsense. Tony wasn't quite sure he believed it, but he sure as shit wasn't going to let any of the guys hurt Bridget's feelings by making fun of her.

Finally, Chris shrugged. "Psych gets feelings that usually save our butts. Why not ghosts?"

Travis pursed his lips. "'There are more things in heaven and earth, Horatio, than are dreamt of in your philosophy.'"

Everyone turned to look at him.

"What?" Travis frowned. "I read, assholes."

Willow buried her face in his shoulder, her sides heaving.

"Well, whatever it was, I'm just glad you're okay." Caroline raised her glass to Bridget. "And if there are spirits, Kieran definitely would have been an avenging one, doing whatever he could to protect you."

"How's Patty?" Willow asked.

"Coming back to work in a week." Bridget looped her arm around Tony's neck, and his chest warmed. He loved how comfortable they were with each other. Like they'd been together for years. "She had a concussion and some bruised ribs, but she'll be fine."

Bridget's breast pressed into his pec muscles. She was warm and soft and suddenly he didn't want to share her with their friends. "Dance?" he asked.

She blinked in surprise, but nodded. He lifted her off his lap and led her to the wood dance floor in the corner of the bar. He ignored the fast beat of the music and pulled her into his arms.

"This is our first dance." Bridget wrapped her arms around his waist and leaned her cheek against his chest.

He sighed. The moment, the woman, were perfect. He couldn't believe what an idiot he'd been not willing to give them a chance.

"There's been so much going on with police interviews and moving Patty into one of Chris's properties that we haven't had much time to just relax and talk." He rested his chin on the top of her head and inhaled the sweet scent of her shampoo. "That night, before he grabbed you, I wanted you to meet someone important to me. And then my ex came up and—"

"I didn't think that was who you wanted me to meet. You would never be so cruel to shove a girlfriend in my face."

"But you left—"

"I left because I didn't want to go to jail again for assault. I wanted to claw her eyes out." Bridget leaned back and met his eyes. She smiled. "She was touching what was mine. And I can't have another arrest on my record."

"I don't know." Relief coursed through him. He had enough to make up for with this woman; he didn't need to add things he hadn't been guilty of to the list. "I kind of like that I'm with a bad girl. I'll never be bored." He slid his hand down her lower back and squeezed.

"The bad girl and the boy scout?" She tilted her head. "It has a certain ring. But you'll have to settle for the nerd and the Raider."

"You should know by now that I don't settle." He pushed a curl off her face. "I got exactly what I wanted."

They swayed together for long seconds. Finally, he ran his thumb along her cheekbone. "There's a woman. She lived in the same trailer park as I did. She raised me, really. We're close. I'd like you to meet her."

Bridget's mouth fell open. "You want me to meet your mother?"

"Basically." And he knew it was trite, falling for someone like your mother, but Bridget was a lot like Eloise. No, they didn't dress the same or have the same hobbies, but they both had an inner fire like he'd never seen before. They were both fighters, the only two women who'd ever fought for him. Were both generous and did their best to help the people around them.

She beamed up at him, then her face fell. "Oh God. Then you'll have to meet my parents."

"What, they won't like me?"

"They'll love you," she said glumly. "Fawn all over you. And secretly wonder what I did to trap you into loving me."

"It's not much of a secret." He leaned her over his arm in a slow dip. "You drove me nuts. Made me question every standard I had. Showed me how narrow a world I'd been living in. Made me smile, made me laugh. You brought me to life." He brought his mouth to her ear. "Your smokin' ass doesn't hurt, either."

She slapped his shoulder as he brought her back to standing. But the smile she gave him was everything. It held all his hopes and dreams.

There was a shout, some drunks arguing at a table near the dance floor.

Bridget stepped out of his arms. "I'd better go put a stop to that before it turns into something."

The disagreement was already dying down, one friend patting the other on the back. But Tony knew an opportunity when he saw it. Without hesitation, he bent and tossed Bridget over his shoulder. "No more breaking up bar fights for you." He strode from the *Ginger* amid good-natured hoots and hollers.

He placed her on her feet next to Sheila. She planted her hands on her hips and glared up at him. "You can't just throw me over your shoulder whenever you want."

"Apparently I can." His lips twitched at her outraged huff. She might act offended, but she secretly got a kick out of it.

"I don't know what I'm going to do with you."

"I can think of a few things." And the thought of those things had him hustling her to the door of his car.

She rolled her eyes. "Okay, I can think of some things, too." She went up on tip-toe, her mouth aiming for his when her attention went over his shoulder. "What the...." She ducked under his arm and stalked toward the street. "That man just kicked his dog. Hey!" She waved her arms. "Tampon licker! What the hell do you think you're doing?"

Tony shook his head. His fun time would have to wait. But watching Bridget when she went on one of her tears could be almost as amusing.

He went after her, quickening his step to get between the man and his woman.

Because where Bridget was concerned, he never knew what could happen.

Also By Allyson Charles

Hunted

Stalked

Burnt

Ghosted

Putting Out Old Flames

Under the Christmas Tree

Courting Disaster

All Wrapped Up

Shelter Me

Forever Home

Forever Found

Forever Wild

The Bakeshop at Pumpkin and Spice(with Donna Kauff-man and Kate Angell)

A Wedding on Bluebird Way (with Lori Wilde, Janey Dai-ley, and Stacey Keith)

That Mistletoe Moment (with Cat Johnson and Kate An-gell)

About Allyson Charles

Allyson Charles lives in Colorado. She's the author of sexy and funny small-town romances, and steamy and fast-paced military romances. A former attorney, she happily ditched those suits and now works in her pajamas writing about men's briefs instead of legal briefs. When she's not writing, she's probably engaged in one of her favorite hobbies: napping, eating, or martial arts (That last one almost makes up for the first two, right?). One of Allyson's greatest sources of happiness is that she now lives in a city that has a Cracker Barrel.

Allyson Charles also writes steamy historical romances under the name Alyson Chase, and paranormal romances under the name A. Caprice.

You can find her at www.allysoncharles.com.

Printed in Great Britain
by Amazon

44930211R00130